"You can't save Jordan?"

Anger and despair warred in his blue eyes and held her in her seat. And behind that she sensed a parent in need of something. She'd seen it too many times in the E.R.

She leaned forward and clasped her hands over his. "I can't, but you can. Maybe. If you're a match."

What if he contested the adoption? What if he sued for custody? Yanking her hands away from his, she clenched them together and held them on the table by sheer force. What she wanted to do was bang them up and down to relieve the tension exploding inside her. Elizabeth wondered how long she had to stay. Her feet already pointed toward the door and it wouldn't take much to convince them to flee.

"What do you want from me, Blake?" Elizabeth forced the words through clenched teeth.

"To see my daughter. To be her father."

Books by Kim Watters

Love Inspired

On Wings of Love
Home Sweet Home
And Father Makes Three

KIM WATTERS

At twelve years old, Kim fell in love with romance after she borrowed a Harlequin Romance book from her older sister's bookshelf. An avid reader, she was soon hooked on the happily-ever-after endings. For years she dreamed of writing her own romance novel, but never had the time until she moved from the hustle and bustle of Chicago to a small town north of Phoenix, Arizona.

Kim still lives in that same small town with her two wonderful children, three cats and one neurotic hamster.

And Father Makes Three

Kim Watters

Love Inspired

Recycling programs
for this product may
not exist in your area.

™ LOVE INSPIRED BOOKS

ISBN-13: 978-0-373-87756-0

AND FATHER MAKES THREE

www.LoveInspiredBooks.com

Printed in U.S.A.

I will lead the blind by ways they have not known;
along unfamiliar paths I will guide them;
I will turn the darkness into light before them
and make the rough places smooth.
These are the things I will do; I will not forsake them.
—*Isaiah* 42:16

For Carol Herra and her entire support team.
They never gave up, and through the grace of God,
Carol is here today with us because of
the willingness of a bone marrow donor.

I'd like to thank the following groups and staff
for all their help with my research for this book.

The Leukemia and Lymphoma Society, www.lls.org/

Be The Match Foundation, www.marrow.org/

The National Marrow Donor Program,
www.marrow.org/

And all the others who tirelessly answered
my questions and didn't want to be named. Thanks.
I couldn't have done it without you.

Disclaimer: Any errors or inaccuracies contained
within this are the sole responsibility of the author
and not of the organizations listed above.

Chapter One

"Dr. Randall? Dr. Elizabeth Randall?" Pulling her focus from the patient chart in front of her, Elizabeth Randall snapped her attention to the tall man next to her. Anger simmered beneath her calm facade as she took in his brown hair and strong jawline covered with a hint of a five o'clock shadow. Under any other circumstances, she might have found the stranger attractive.

Not now.

"Yes. I was wondering when you'd get here."

It was about time someone from Child Protective Services showed up. Mario Martinez-Alvarez had been at Agnes P. Kingfisher Memorial Hospital in Scottsdale, Arizona, just under two hours waiting for a caseworker to appear. The child's black eye and broken ribs had not been caused by a simple fall from a high chair. Mario's stepfather had been taken into custody and the mother had yet to be found.

Unlike some, Mario would recover, but each time a young innocent victim came through the hospital doors, her heart broke at the injustice. Children were precious. A gift from God that some people took for granted.

Not Elizabeth. Her fingers tightened on the pen in her hand until it became painful.

"Excuse me? You know why I'm here?"

"Of course. The boy has been transferred upstairs. Dr. Harris is his attending now." After signing her name, Elizabeth closed the chart and turned slightly so she could rest against the nurses' station. She took in the man's casual clothing—a dark blue Phoenix Fire Department T-shirt and jeans. In all her experience with CPS caseworkers, she'd yet to come across one dressed so casually, who didn't carry a briefcase or at least a notebook or day planner of some sort.

Maybe she'd been hasty in her assessment. "You are with CPS, aren't you?"

Uncertainty clouded his blue eyes as he shifted his weight. "No, I work for the City of Phoenix Fire Department."

"Oh. Sorry." Elizabeth softened her tone, feeling guilty for letting her bad day affect her work. It wasn't his fault her adopted daughter, Jordan, had developed another infection at her IV site. Crossing her arms, she gave the man her full attention. Concern furrowed the lightly tanned skin on his forehead. "How may I help you then, Mr.…?"

"Blake Crawford. Blake William Crawford."

He spoke his name as if she should know him. He looked vaguely familiar now. If he worked for the fire department, it was quite possible she'd seen him bring in a patient or two, but they'd never been formally introduced. She'd remember meeting someone like him.

She grasped his extended hand, surprised to feel a slight connection. She shook it off as fatigue.

"Dr. Elizabeth Randall. But you knew that. I'm afraid I'm at a disadvantage here."

"I need to talk to you about my daughter."

"Your daughter?" No female children had been brought into the E.R. today and she'd already met the fathers of the few who had come in over the past week. None of them were Blake Crawford. "I don't believe I've met your daughter. When was she brought in?"

"She wasn't."

"Then I'm afraid I can't help you. Have you spoken to her pediatrician?"

"I have no idea who her pediatrician is. She doesn't live with me." He ran a hand through his short, cropped hair as his gaze darted around the area before it returned to her. "She's with you."

Elizabeth felt the blood drain from her face and she forgot to breathe. That meant—impossible. Nobody knew the identity of Jordan's biological father. Not even her. She gasped, trying to fill her lungs with air.

A few doctors and nurses milled around the nurses' station, watching them with interest as they waited for new patients to arrive. Elizabeth wondered if she was being set up. She glanced at the nurse behind the desk. Lidia busied herself with some paperwork and refused to look up. That was it.

This had all the makings of a great April Fool's Day and birthday prank.

No one got through their special day in the E.R. without some sort of recognition. At least they hadn't sent a singing telegram like they had with Dr. Kennedy, or worse like they had with Dr. Emory. But this was cruel. Especially with Jordan's precarious health. Someone would get a good talking to when Blake fessed up. "Which one of my coworkers put you up to this?"

"No one put me up to this. This isn't a prank." He reached out to her, but stopped short. "I have every reason to believe my daughter is living with you."

One by one, her coworkers took off in various directions without so much as a word. Dread pounded in her veins. The hard edge of the counter bit into her back, so Elizabeth adjusted her position. But nothing seemed comfortable as long as the man who believed he was her daughter's biological father remained in her view with expectation written in his eyes.

Until she figured out if there was any real truth to this story, this was one conversation she did not want her coworkers to hear. Rumors and gossip blew through the hospital like an out-of-control dust storm, and she didn't need Jordan hearing the news and getting her hopes up. They had enough to deal with already.

"Come with me." Gently taking his arm, she led him outside the E.R. toward the towering mesquite tree where the administration had placed a wrought-iron bench in memory of her late husband, Dr. Thomas Randall. Tom. The love of her life. She could sure use his guidance right now because sitting there with another man who claimed to be their daughter's biological father didn't feel right, but her only other choice was the noisy cafeteria at lunchtime.

She motioned for Blake to sit yet she remained standing. Folding her arms, she watched him hunker down and wedge his elbows against his knees. A horn honked in the distance and the constant thrum of traffic blended in with the coo of the pigeons as the sunlight glistened off the palm trees lining 92nd Street.

"What makes you think your daughter is with me?"

"Does the name Tessa Pruitt ring a bell?"

Tessa Pruitt! "Should it?"

"Yes. She was the mother of my child."

Panic churned the coffee in her stomach. No one else knew the name of Jordan's birth mother. Not even Elizabeth's best friend, Susie. This wasn't a joke.

But Tessa had told Elizabeth she didn't know who Jordan's father was. Why had she lied all these years?

Elizabeth yearned to sprint away from the madness surrounding her. Run until her lungs burned and her muscles screamed in protest. But she couldn't. She had a job to do and a daughter to care for. Elizabeth's stomach lurched as she sank down on the bench next to him and covered her face with her hands. "Tessa was one of my best friends. But what makes you think you're her daughter's father?"

"She sent me a letter." Blake turned his head and studied the tall, thin woman with short, dark, wavy hair wearing light blue scrubs printed with colorful crayons and a lab coat. Her long, delicate fingers cradled her face, hiding it from his view.

What was she thinking?

He'd had a week to come to terms with the knowledge he was a father. Apparently he'd blindsided Dr. Randall with the news. She probably thought she'd get to keep his child. Tiredness swept over him and he ran his hand across his face. Last night's paintball marathon with his old high school buddy, Eric Stevens, was best left to the teenagers they used to be, not thirty-somethings who should know better. Blake paid the price today.

An ambulance pulled out from the overhang by the E.R. doors. A Scottsdale team, not Phoenix, but it didn't matter—they shared a camaraderie nonetheless. He nodded to the driver as he went by. Coming to see Dr. Randall at work probably hadn't been the smartest move, but he had no other contact information.

He had to see for himself if there was any truth to Tessa's story. From Dr. Randall's stunned reaction, his ex-wife's words were true. Hope surged—the girl was his only remaining family member. Despite his fears about parenting, he wanted to meet this child and be a part of her life.

Blake stood and scratched the back of his neck as he paced the dusty-brown earth in front of the bench. Brittle mesquite beans crunched under his feet. "You know Tessa died three months ago."

"Yes, from a ruptured brain aneurysm. We always remained friends even though she decided med school wasn't her thing after her first year." A tear slid down Elizabeth's cheek.

"Yeah, med school wasn't my thing, either." Blake

reached out, but stopped short of wiping the moisture away. He didn't like the effect this woman had on him. He hadn't had a reaction like this since Tessa. And look where that relationship had ended up.

A moment of silence lingered between the two.

"It's not for everybody." He watched Elizabeth dry her cheeks and regain her composure. "The last time I saw her was right after Christmas two weeks before she died. I knew something was wrong. Her forgetfulness—or spells, as she called them—had become a lot more frequent and her headaches much worse. But she blew off my concerns and focused more than usual on Jordan, as if she suspected something. If only I'd known."

"It wouldn't have mattered. Tessa lived by her own rules. When she made up her mind about something, no one could change it." He tapped his thumb against his jean-clad knee. Something didn't add up. Dr. Randall didn't know him, or anything about him, and yet his child was with her. Tessa had always had a secretive side to her and liked to play games. Apparently nothing had changed.

Blake reached into his pocket and pulled out the letter from his ex-wife. It weighed only an ounce, but felt like a ton. The cryptic knowledge it contained had changed his life completely last week, as it would the woman's sitting next to him. Tessa's words on the crisp linen stationery days before her death bound them together.

He handed her the envelope. "Here. This will explain things."

He'd learned of Tessa's death through her attorney a

week ago. Sadness burned the blood in his veins. The grief he'd seen on countless faces as an EMT and fireman for the Phoenix Fire Department clouded his vision. Gone. Dead. He'd loved her, or thought he'd had, but in the end, they were just another statistic.

Unsure if his legs could carry his weight, Blake sat back down next to Elizabeth, making sure to keep as much distance between them as the bench allowed. As she pulled out the paper, he wedged his elbows against his knees, and stared down at an ant carrying a huge crumb, reminding him that struggle was everywhere in life.

He attempted to fill his lungs with much-needed air. As he squeezed his eyes shut, an image of Tessa appeared behind his lids as it had every day since he'd learned of her death. Her long, mocha-colored hair contrasted with her milky-white skin. Her warm, generous smile and chocolate-brown eyes along with her positive outlook on life had shone a ray of hope into the darkness consuming him.

His inability to allow anyone to get really close to him had caused him to blow the best thing that had ever happened in his life.

Now all that remained was a child that he had no idea how to be a father to. He'd better learn quickly. And Tessa had made sure the woman sitting beside him would help. That must be why she'd left his daughter with her.

"I don't understand this." Elizabeth stared at him, shock registering in her light blue eyes as she inhaled sharply. Her fingers strangled the stethoscope around her neck until her knuckles gleamed in the bright April sunshine. The moisture gathering in her eyes added another layer of depth to her character, and it rocked him.

"My ex-wife was obviously pregnant when we split up. She had a child and decided not to tell me until after her death."

"She said she didn't know who the father was. She never told me she'd been married."

"We never told anyone. It didn't last long enough." Remorse filled him.

Blake took the letter back, scanning the contents again to make sure he hadn't missed anything. His fingers shook as he took in her slanted, curvy handwriting, which she obviously struggled to create.

Blake,

I hope this letter finds you well. There are two things I want to tell you and I know I don't have a lot of time left. My brain aneurysm is inoperable and my symptoms are getting worse, which is why I'm putting my affairs in order.

I actually find it kind of ironic that I would die first when you were the one who always took the risks, but such is life. I've found God and have been praying daily to find answers, and I've finally found peace. I hope you will someday, too. I love you. I always did, always will.

First, I'm sorry I ran out on our marriage, but I only wanted you to be happy. I couldn't give you what you needed. I hope some day you find someone who can, if you haven't already.

Second, you are a father. Your daughter is with Elizabeth Randall, who works at Kingfisher Memorial in Scottsdale. Since I cannot be a part of her life anymore, I'm passing on that responsibility to you.

I'm sorry I never told you, and am only doing so with a letter, but I was a coward then, and things still haven't changed. I suppose I could have found you all those years ago, but I did what I thought best for both of you. I can only hope you'll forgive me when you see what a beautiful daughter we created. A daughter who needs you. They both do. Please go to them now that you've read this letter and love your daughter like I did. Elizabeth can answer any other questions you might have.

With love,
Tessa

Nothing had changed since the day he'd received it. What he couldn't figure out was why Tessa's attorney had waited over two months to contact him, or why Elizabeth needed his help. He knew why he needed hers.

He was a father. No longer the last of the Crawfords in this line.

Blake folded the paper back up and tucked it into his pocket again. "What's her name?"

"Tessa named her Jordan."

"Jordan?" Somehow Blake managed to keep his voice low and even. Jordan had been his mother's maiden name. Tessa truly had loved him in spite of his flaws. So why had she left him? And why had she kept the knowledge of their daughter's existence from him?

This whole conversation was surreal. He'd come to meet the woman who had Jordan so he could make arrangements to see her. Take her home with him. Learn to be a good father, not like the one who'd raised him. And yet fear gripped his heart.

This couldn't have happened at a worse time. With his schedule, how could he take care of a child? Who would watch her when he pulled his twenty-four-hour shifts? He'd have to buy a bigger condo, or maybe even a house. What did he even know about kids anyway, especially preteen girls?

None of that mattered. He'd figure it out. "When can I pick her up?"

"Pick her up?" Confusion filled Elizabeth's voice, followed by compassion. "I'm sorry, Blake, but Jordan's my daughter now. My late husband and I adopted her."

"What? When?"

"At birth."

"Wait a minute. At birth? So why— This doesn't make any sense." He jumped up and began to pace, leaving a trail in the dirt.

"I'm sorry you were sent here on a wild-goose chase, Blake. I have no idea why Tessa would be so cruel to either one of us."

Sirens sounded in the distance and Elizabeth's phone chirped. He knew she was wrestling with wanting to be in two places at once. Her patients depended on her, but this was an important conversation. Her gaze flipped between the hospital and him.

"This is far from over."

"What do you want from me, Blake?"

Elizabeth rose to her full height, which almost matched his, and drilled him with her gaze. But he refused to be intimidated by the doctor.

"I want my daughter."

"So who was the dude in the blue T-shirt?" Susie Tan stared at Elizabeth over the rim of her coffee cup in the hospital cafeteria a few hours later. The nurse's lips formed a straight line. "You looked upset when you returned."

"Jordan's biological father."

"Whoa. Wait a minute. He's what?" Susie's eyebrows rose and her mouth dropped open.

Elizabeth's fingers tightened around the foam coffee cup. "Jordan's father. Apparently the mother lied about not knowing his identity. They were married at the time of Jordan's conception."

"Oh, Elizabeth, I'm so sorry. What does he want?" Marcella Rodriguez from the Labor & Delivery department asked.

"Jordan." Elizabeth barely contained the sob in her voice.

"Does he know?" Susie questioned.

"No." Elizabeth took a sip of her coffee and scalded her tongue. She closed her eyes and shifted in the hard, plastic chair. How would Blake react to his daughter's illness? Would it make him go away and leave them alone?

Wrong. That wasn't fair of her.

"What I don't get is why now? Why didn't he come forward years ago?"

"He just found out."

"Do you suppose he knows something you don't?" Marcella flipped open the tab of her diet soda, worry creasing her brow. "I mean, I know you won't want to hear this, but are you sure the adoption was legal? I'd think he would have had to sign off on it, which means he knew about his ex-wife's pregnancy. The fact he didn't…"

Elizabeth inhaled sharply and opened her eyes. Ice momentarily chilled her veins. As if she didn't have enough to worry about. She dragged in a painful breath as his last words rang in her ears. "I want my daughter!"

"Hey, I'm sure the adoption was legal." Susie interjected. "You know this might work in your favor. A father without all the complications, and it would be nice for you to have someone else to help you through this."

"Knights in shining armor only appear in fairy tales. I'd still make sure about the adoption. My cousin knows an adoption attorney—he handled their adoption last year." Concern now laced Marcella's voice as she ripped open a candy bar and popped a piece of chocolate into her mouth. "I'll get Arturo's work number for you unless you can track down the original attorney."

"It's probably not necessary, but thanks. I'd appreciate that." Elizabeth toyed with the salt and pepper shakers on the table to keep her fingers from trembling. Every once in a while—like today—memories of the day she adopted Jordan haunted her. Had she done the right thing all those years ago when she came up with a solution for Tessa's pregnancy? What if the adoption wasn't legal after all? What if Blake decided he wanted custody?

What if she lost Jordan in another way?

An uncomfortable silence lingered at the table as Marcella finished up her snack and Susie fingered the red-and-white stir stick in her coffee cup. "So who's up to seeing a movie Friday night?"

"I am. Are you, Elizabeth? You could use a night out."

Elizabeth unwound her fingers from the shakers and forced a smile to her lips. "Sure. After I get Jordan to sleep."

Susie crushed Marcella's candy wrapper and stuffed it inside her empty coffee cup. "Sounds like a plan."

Elizabeth's phone chirped, signaling a text. Pulling out her BlackBerry, she glanced at the message and sighed. "Gotta run. Jordan's doctor wants to see me."

"—I pray the Lord my soul to keep. Amen."

"Amen." As Elizabeth gently squeezed her nine-year-old daughter's hand, anxiety twisted her muscles into a knot. Jordan had lost more weight and her bald spots were more prominent from her last round of chemo. Soon they'd have to shave off the rest of her shoulder-length, dark brown hair. Elizabeth contained the sob in her throat. Jordan had to get better.

Please, God, heal my daughter.

Still kneeling beside her hospital bed, Jordan lifted her head and gazed out the window. Elizabeth knew she looked into the twilight, pretending to see God's face smiling down at her. While Elizabeth didn't have her daughter's imagination and would only see the darkening horizon, the outline of another building to the left of the hospital and the silhouette of Camelback Mountain in the distance, she still felt His love, and the emerging twinkling stars filled her with hope.

While her faith hadn't waned over the course of Jordan's illness, the trips to the hospital and doctors' offices had superseded attending church. That was going to change. Just yesterday, she'd again seen the power of belief when a five-year-old accident victim came through the E.R. doors and the family and friends kept up a silent vigil during the successful three-hour surgery.

Another quick prayer slipped through Elizabeth's lips.

With the decreasing activity on the children's floor of the hospital, stillness crept into the room. Elizabeth massaged her daughter's bony shoulders. So far this bout of leukemia had robbed Jordan of three months of a normal childhood. Yet some of the other children on the floor faced far worse battles. She prayed that they would find a compatible bone-marrow donor and that the doctors here would find cures for the rest of the children.

"Now in bed with you." Elizabeth helped her daughter slide between the white sheets and settle against her favorite purple-and-pink butterfly pillow. Elizabeth sat on the side of the bed and leaned over to give her a kiss. "Good night, sweetpea. I love you."

"Good night, Mom. I love you, too."

Elizabeth caressed Jordan's cheek. So soft, so innocent, so young. This illness had to be part of God's plan. He'd drawn her into medicine so that she could assist others, and with His help, she'd find a way to save her daughter.

But did that include Blake Crawford?

Elizabeth folded back the blanket and smoothed out the creases. "We'll get through this, Jordan. I promise."

"I know. We did before." Jordan gave her a tired grin.

"Yes, we did. And this time, we'll make sure it doesn't come back." Rising to her feet, Elizabeth turned off the lights and left the room. Once outside, she leaned against the wall.

Maintaining a positive attitude around Jordan drained her. Overhead, the fluorescent lights dimmed, signaling the end of visiting hours. The harsh, institutional glare made her miss the warm, inviting atmosphere of their two-bedroom townhome. A townhome which stood vacant now because Elizabeth had moved into the doctors' quarters downstairs while her daughter remained in the hospital.

If only Blake knew how close he was to Jordan when he came to see her today. Did he really want his daughter? Was there anything she could do to stop him?

She squeezed her eyelids shut, glad the hallway was empty. The sound of rustling sheets inside Jordan's room caught her attention and Elizabeth strained to hear her daughter's soft, tired voice floating into the hallway.

"Please, God, bring me another daddy before I die. Then Mommy won't be so lonely anymore. Good night."

Before I die.

Jordan had lost her will to live, and they still had a long way to go to beat the leukemia. Dipping her head, Elizabeth lost her hard-won composure. She bit her lip as a tear slid down her cheek. Jordan's nightly prayer still hadn't changed, not that she expected it would.

Had God been listening? Is that why Blake had shown up when he did? Or did his appearance have another meaning—one that might not have a happy-ever-after ending after all?

Chapter Two

"Let's go." Blake motioned to his partner, Corey Abrahamson, the following morning. He wheeled the stretcher toward the emergency room doors that led outside to the waiting ambulance. The accident had been a fender bender, yet they'd brought the elderly man to the hospital to be checked over as a precaution.

Now that the call was over, Blake had nothing but time on his hands and a daughter on his mind. He helped Corey lift the stretcher into the back of the ambulance, figuring that Elizabeth Randall was off today because he hadn't seen her in the E.R. Maybe she was with a patient.

Suddenly he realized that outside Kingfisher, he had no way of contacting her. After closing and securing the doors, he pulled a piece of paper out of his pocket and quickly scribbled a note.

"Hang on. I forgot something." He strode back through the doors and left the note with the nurse behind the desk. Elizabeth wouldn't get his phone number until Monday, but there was nothing he could do about that. Sweet-talking the young intern had only resulted in finding out the doctor's next shift.

A doctor. Now that he'd met the woman and reality was setting in, dread pounded in his heart. Tessa had given their daughter up for adoption to a doctor.

Not that his late ex-wife would have known about his aversion to doctors, because they'd met in med school when Blake was still trying to gain his father's approval. In their whirlwind courtship and brief marriage, Dr. William Crawford—the cutting-edge heart surgeon— had never been mentioned. It didn't take long for Blake to realize he didn't want to be a doctor, and he quit. After Tessa left him, he enlisted in the army instead of returning home to face his father's wrath. And right about that time, he started living for the moment and seeking out every thrill he could find. While others went out and saved the world, he spent his money and time trying to save himself from the demons of his youth. With a daughter now, he had to start thinking of someone else. It rocked him to the core.

"All set now?" Corey leaned against the side of the ambulance.

"Yes." Blake strode to the driver's side of the cab. Once inside, he snapped his seat belt into place and flipped the switch to let dispatch know they were available for another call. Blake pulled air into his lungs, yet suffocation still threatened to pull him under. "What's it like being a dad?"

His question startled the other man. No surprise there—sports and food usually dominated their conversations.

Corey gave him a dubious look.

"Did Karen put you up to this?"

"No."

Blake started the engine, put the ambulance in drive and pulled out into the parking lot. Once the numbness had worn off, the anticipation he'd felt earlier when he'd read the letter from Tessa returned. Another generation of Crawfords existed. Responsibility weighed on his shoulders, but he knew the right thing to do. He would meet Jordan and be a part of her life, despite the adoption. Dr. Randall couldn't keep him from her forever.

But what would happen then? Apprehension gripped his heart.

Would Jordan reject him like everyone else in his life?

"I just found out last week I'm a father."

"How'd you find out?" His partner whistled as Blake stopped the ambulance at a red light. As he tapped the steering wheel impatiently, waiting for the signal to change, both Tessa's and Elizabeth's faces rose in his mind's eye. How different they were, yet his late ex-wife had changed his life in one way, and the doctor would as well when she allowed him to see Jordan. "I received a letter from my ex-wife's attorney last week."

"I never knew you were married."

"Not many people do. It's not one of the highlights of my life." Blake sighed.

"What happened?"

"We were too young. I didn't understand what it took to be a good husband. Tessa probably didn't have any confidence in me as a father either, because after she split she never told me she was pregnant." Blake hit the gas and stared out the window as streets and houses replaced strip malls. Tension tightened his neck muscles and bracketed his mouth. "I want to meet her, but I'm scared I'll blow it. I don't know how to do it. What's it like?"

Corey didn't answer until they'd stopped at another light. "I think you'd make a good father. You're there for people when they need it and that's what matters. This'll sound cliché, but being a parent is one of the most rewarding and frustrating jobs there is. There's no instruction manual, you just kind of wing it."

That was the problem. He'd had no relationship with his father and had no idea how to start. His daughter was almost ten years old—the past had already been repeated.

A strange emotion pulled at his heart when he thought about the daughter he had yet to meet. An unbreakable bond had been set in place the moment he'd received the letter. In an instant, clarity whacked him and he gripped the steering wheel like a lifeline.

Blowing it with Jordan was only the beginning of his worries.

"Have a second?" Blake knocked on the partially open door to Dr. Eric Stevens's office inside Kingfisher Memorial Hospital late Tuesday afternoon. He thought Elizabeth would have contacted him by now, but apparently not. He glanced at his cell phone again to see if he'd missed a call. Nothing.

The woman couldn't avoid him forever. As Jordan's

biological father, he should have some rights, even if someone else had adopted his daughter.

Surprise shone in his paintball buddy's eyes. "Sure. Come in. Ready to talk about your defeat?"

"I'll challenge you to a rematch anytime you're ready." Striding into the room, Blake suffered déjà vu. His late father's office had been laid out the same way, even though it was farther down the hall. All the hours he'd spent inside this building after middle school crowded his brain, and anxiety twisted his stomach. Blake had spent most of his time reading his father's books and trailing after medical staff to learn the ropes.

Other twelve-year-olds were playing basketball, while he was watching open-heart surgery.

Blake sank down in a chair before his knees gave out. He'd fainted during that procedure, a fact his father never let him forget. Beads of sweat formed on his upper lip and forehead.

Outside of the E.R., Blake hadn't stepped foot in the deep interior of Kingfisher again until today.

"What brings you to my neck of the woods, then?" Eric pulled his glasses from his face and set them down on the file he'd been reading, tipping back in his chair. Piles of research files and books leaned dangerously to one side and three half-empty foam cups lined the edge, ready to topple into the overflowing garbage can.

Having grown up blocks from each other, his best friend knew more about Blake than anyone. Even Tessa, which was probably another problem in their marriage. Instead of talking, Blake kept things bottled up. The less people knew, the less chance of his getting hurt.

"Dr. Randall. You know her?"

Eric eyed him warily. "Sure. But she hardly interacts with anyone outside the E.R. Why?"

Sweat rolled down Blake's forehead. "Her daughter is mine."

"What?" The front legs of Eric's battered chair thudded against the carpeted floor. "Jordan is yours? How did that happen? I didn't know you knew Elizabeth all those years ago." His eyes widened as he stared at Blake from the other side of his small, cramped desk.

"I didn't know her. She adopted Jordan from my ex-wife."

"Wow." Eric fingered a vintage World War I model airplane on the only part of his desk that wasn't buried under mounds of stuff. Deftly, he avoided Blake's gaze.

"Wait a minute. If she doesn't interact with anyone here, how do you know about Jordan?" Blake wanted to grab the sleek yellow bi-winged plane from his friend's hands and force him to concentrate on the conversation. Things hadn't changed much since high school, and Eric was still the master of dodging uncomfortable situations. He spun the propeller around with his pointer finger and stared at it intently.

"Despite Dr. Randall's attempts to keep it private, nothing goes unnoticed by the staff. Especially because Jordan is being treated here."

"What do you mean she's being treated here?" The blood drained from Blake's face. "What's wrong with her?"

"Dr. Randall didn't tell you?"

"No. What's wrong with my daughter? Tell me."

Blake curled his fingers around the arms of his chair to keep from jumping up.

Eric dusted the empty spot on the desk with his palm before he put the plane back. Then he leaned back, the front legs of his chair off the floor again. "We watch each other's backs here at Kingfisher. I can't. I've said too much as it is. Dr. Randall will have to tell you herself." Compassion filled Eric's eyes. "I'm sorry, Blake, in more ways than one. Life stinks sometimes."

"Tell me about it." Tension bit into Blake's shoulder muscles, still a tad sore from their recent paintball excursion. "Dr. Randall has a lot of explaining to do, if I can get a few minutes of her time."

Eric steepled his fingers together underneath his chin. "Because we have a history of running wild together and my dad bailed you out of a few scrapes, there are a few other things you need to know about Dr. Randall."

"Like what?" Having grown up with a doctor, Blake didn't think anything could surprise him.

"She's a genius who intimidates everyone on staff. Me included. My dad's the only one who isn't intimidated by her, but then again he's been here forever. He's retiring—they're throwing a party for him Saturday night. You should stop by. He'd like to see you again."

"Dr. Randall sounds like my father," Blake said, ignoring his friend's attempt to change the subject.

"Dr. Randall did a fast track. She graduated from Harvard at twenty-two and finished her residency before most students get through med school. Most people her age are just getting their feet wet in a hospital setting, not passing their five-year anniversary mark."

"I can handle that." Blake stood. "She's working today, isn't she?"

Eric made a quick call. "If you wander down to the E.R., you'll run in to her, but her shift's almost over. I'm not done yet." He paused and eyed Blake warily. "She's also the widow of the late renowned heart surgeon Thomas Randall."

Thomas Randall. *The* Thomas Randall? The name conjured up a big, black hole in Blake's heart. His father had mentored Thomas Randall, but he'd died young, much to his father's grief. In Dr. Crawford's eyes, Tommy had been the son Blake would never be. And now that his father was gone, Blake would never have the chance to prove otherwise.

He squeezed the bridge of his nose. How could Tessa give away his child to Thomas Randall? All work and no play left no time for any family time. No matter how many times Blake had begged his father to play ball with him or come to one of his games, his dad was too busy helping others.

Resentment, anger and disappointment fought for dominance. Blake didn't know what type of mother Elizabeth was, but his daughter would not suffer the same lonely existence he had. With Thomas Randall dead, Jordan needed a father.

And not just any man that Elizabeth might be involved with. Jordan needed her real father. Now.

"Are you okay?" Eric's question brought him back to the present.

"Thanks for the info, I'll see you around." He strode to the door and shot his friend a quick smile as he marched into the hallway, determined to find Elizabeth Randall.

Her shift over, Elizabeth wanted to grab a quick bite before she went upstairs to visit Jordan. As she headed out the E.R. doors, her head down, she crashed into someone.

"Oh, excuse me," said a warm, masculine voice.

"No, excuse me. My fault. I wasn't looking where I was going." She looked up and found herself face-to-face with Blake Crawford. He was better looking than she'd remembered. His short, cropped brown hair accented the smooth planes of his cheeks and his strong jawline covered with a hint of a five o'clock shadow. Dimples creased his cheeks and laugh lines crowded the corners of his eyes despite the fact that he wore a frown.

"Blake?" Jordan's father was on the receiving end of her inability to stay focused on her surroundings. Not good. As a doctor, she needed to be aware of what went on around her. What if she screwed up in triage? What if she made a life-threatening mistake?

Jordan's health had started to affect her ability to remain calm and composed. Wouldn't the head nurse love to see unflappable Dr. Randall right now? Her skin prickled. The anxiety she felt when she first held the tiny infant in her arms almost ten years ago resurfaced. At that time, though, she'd had Tom to help her. Was it possible that Blake Crawford could fill in and take over the role of father like Jordan wanted?

There could only be one reason why Blake had come today: to confront her. He must have found out the truth about her part in the adoption, and he'd come to try to take Jordan away. She'd fight him every step of the way.

"I'm thirsty. Care to join me?" Not giving her a choice, Blake took her arm and led her into the cafeteria.

Five minutes later, after grabbing their food, Blake spoke her name as if testing it out. "Elizabeth Randall. Sorry to hear about your husband."

"You knew Tom?"

"Only by reputation." His words had an edge to them.

"Thank you." Elizabeth wished she was privy to whatever thoughts or ideas whirled around inside his brain. Everyone liked Tom. To her knowledge, her husband had never caused that type of reaction before.

"So what kind of doctor are you?"

His question surprised her. "A pediatric emergency room doctor."

After sending up a quick, silent prayer of thanks for her meal, she bit into her sandwich, not surprised it had no taste. None of the cafeteria food really did.

"So you only help kids."

"Yes, unless I happen to be the only doctor available." Pain radiated from Elizabeth's core. While she helped others, Jordan's cure remained out of her reach, and it killed her to watch the leukemia gain an upper hand. She had to have faith that God knew what He was doing. Maybe bringing Jordan's father into her life could tip the scales in the right direction. She noticed Blake eyeing her, as if sensing her inner turmoil.

"That must be a tough gig."

"It has its moments, but it's also very rewarding at the end of the day." Dragging in a ragged breath, she prayed for strength to get through the rest of the night. Jordan's fever had broken late this afternoon, but she wasn't out of danger.

A family of four helped themselves to food from the vending machine stationed near the rear of the cafeteria. The girl, dressed in basketball attire, looked to be a few years older than Jordan. Would her daughter ever be healthy enough to play sports or visit with her friends? Yes. Elizabeth would make certain that happened. The leukemia would go into remission again, and Jordan would grow up and become the veterinarian she wanted to be.

"So can you help Jordan?" Questions filled his blue eyes and held her in her seat.

"I'm not sure I know what you're talking about." Elizabeth fought to breathe. What did Blake know about Jordan?

"Really? You have nothing at all to tell me about my daughter? Like that she's sick?"

Elizabeth felt the blood leave her cheeks. Light-headed, she reached out for the table, but her hand connected with the Blake's. "Who told you?"

Blake ignored her question, taking her hand. "What's wrong with her?"

She tried to extricate herself from his grasp. He only tightened his grip.

"Jordan has leukemia. It's come out of remission."

"Leukemia?"

"Yes." Elizabeth's voice trembled, leaving the rest

of the sentence unspoken. She closed her eyes to avoid the pain written in his.

"Since Tessa was a part of Jordan's life, she knew about it, didn't she?"

Elizabeth nodded, remembering how despite her own pain, Tessa was there right after they learned of Jordan's relapse. Her friend had been there for her until the end.

"So that's why she said my daughter needed me." Silence filled the space between them.

Grief, anger and regret sucker punched Blake in the gut. Rubbing his eyes, he leaned back in his chair to distance himself. His daughter was dying. He had yet to meet her and he could lose her, too. A renewed sense of urgency took hold. "When do I get to meet Jordan?"

Elizabeth toyed with the straw in her coffee, avoiding his gaze.

"Elizabeth? She's the last of my family. I have every right to meet her. It's what Tessa wanted. It's what I want." Blake squeezed her hands. When she gazed up at him, her light blue eyes shone with fear. In a heartbeat, Blake understood.

She was afraid of losing Jordan. Not only to the leukemia ravaging her body, but to him.

A commotion caught Elizabeth's attention and she stopped one of the E.R. staff as they strode by. "What's going on?"

"Accident. Five on their way in. Three kids."

"I'll be right there." Half-finished cups of coffee and sandwiches were the story of her life, only this time she was glad to leave it behind. Elizabeth's heart raced. She wasn't on duty, but she knew her services would probably be needed for a few hours. She'd make sure to see Jordan before her bedtime.

She rose hastily, scraping the chair on the tile. The lights seemed to grow brighter, magnifying the man next to her. She couldn't avoid Blake's request for long. What if Marcella was right? What if the adoption wasn't legal? What if Blake met his daughter and wanted custody?

"Sorry to cut this short but I'm needed in the E.R. Thanks for dinner."

"This conversation isn't over yet."

Elizabeth held her ground. "It is for now. Please excuse me."

Blake wasn't ready to let the doctor out of his sight. "I'll come with you."

As he escorted her down the hall, he could tell that his words had fallen on deaf ears. Elizabeth had already shut him out, just like his dad used to do. She was his father all over again.

His long strides ate up the tile flooring as he kept pace with the woman. Her face expressionless, he knew she was already in the E.R., mentally going over how to treat her future patients. Neither he nor the janitor polishing the floor existed.

Invisible. Again. Was she this way with their daughter? Suddenly Blake was ten-years-old and waiting for his father to help him build his derby car for the Cub Scout Pack race. A race he never participated in because his block of wood never made it out of the box. His mother had always helped him before, but she'd died ten months earlier from breast cancer. After that, he'd quit scouting like he'd quit almost everything else he'd started in his life.

He wasn't going to quit this time. He wanted to meet his daughter. She was the only thing that tied him to Tessa. "I will meet Jordan, Elizabeth. You can count on that."

"Only on my terms." Her lips drew a straight line. In the distance, he heard the adrenaline-pumping screech of the sirens as the first ambulance pulled in.

He mentally shook himself. Lives stood on the line here. There was no telling how extensive the injuries were. And in her defense, she had been giving him her full attention until the call came in. A piece of understanding wormed its way past the painful memories of his father.

Once inside the E.R., she discarded her purse underneath the desk, then pulled on her lab coat and kept moving.

"Dr. Randall?" A harried nurse stopped short of running into her. She clutched her clipboard to her chest, a look of relief on her face.

"I was in the cafeteria. What are we looking at?"

"An SUV ran a red light and T-boned a car."

Blake felt useless and in the way. He only did fieldwork—basic life support—this wasn't his territory. This was Elizabeth's domain. Why had he insisted on coming?

After marching to the sink, Elizabeth turned on the tap and scrubbed her hands. The sliding doors to their right swooshed open and a paramedic and EMT wheeled in the first patient. After throwing her paper towel away, he watched Elizabeth clasp her hands and bow her head.

"What are you doing?" he asked as another ambulance arrived.

"Praying."

"Praying?" She didn't strike him as the religious type. He wondered if he should tell her prayer didn't really work—if it did, his mother would still be alive.

"Yes. Praying. I don't do my work alone." She strode away from him and never looked back.

Chapter Three

"You should really wait for Dr. Randall before you do this." Eric stopped beside Blake outside room 403. "All it takes is one look and bam, she'll nail you to the wall. I've seen her reduce interns to tears."

"I've met worse. Her bark couldn't be any worse than my dad's. I can handle Dr. Randall."

"Yeah, well, your dad wasn't so good-looking."

Blake looked at Eric, surprised. Dr. Randall was a looker, he couldn't deny that.

"Didn't think you ever noticed women anymore, Eric. You always have your head in a book or worse, glue all over your hands from your model kits."

Eric grinned. "I have my eye on one of the nurses in the E.R."

"Maybe you should live on the edge a bit and ask her out, then."

"Maybe you should call Dr. Randall instead of asking me to sneak you into the Children's Wing." Eric folded his arms across his chest and leaned against the wall.

"We didn't exactly sneak in. I asked and you delivered." Blake flexed his hands as he stood outside of his daughter's room. Getting the visitor badge had been the easy part. The receptionist downstairs hadn't even batted an eye when Eric told her their destination. "My guess is we weren't even in the elevator before the receptionist called the E.R. and told Dr. Randall I was here. I suspect she'll be joining us momentarily."

"Still. This doesn't feel right. What are you going to say to Jordan?"

"Look, I've waited three days for Dr. Randall to call. I've got to force her hand. I deserve to at least see my daughter."

"Maybe she's been busy."

Like Blake's father always had been. Some people should have never been parents.

Did Blake fall into that category? Tessa thought so. Why else had she given Jordan up without consulting him?

Leaning back, Blake allowed the unforgiving wall to bite into his back. Inside the room he heard the drone of the television tuned to some kids' channel.

What did girls like to do? What did they watch? What did they talk about? Blake hadn't thought this through. He couldn't just barge in and say, "Jordan, I am your father."

"Maybe you're right. This wasn't one of my most brilliant moves."

"Look, I've got to get back downstairs. Don't do anything that's going to get me in trouble. In fact, if you're smart, you'll wait for Dr. Randall to call."

"We all know I'm not smart. That's why I dropped out of med school."

"Stop being so hard on yourself."

"I will if you go ask that nurse out."

Eric smiled and headed down the hall. "Good luck, man," he said.

A band of sweat broke out on his forehead despite the air-conditioned temperature inside the hospital. He hovered, unsure of his next move. Just inside the open doorway to his left Jordan Randall lay in a hospital bed, her body ravaged with leukemia. Unlike in his childhood, this time around he understood what cancer was and knew the implications.

What if she didn't make it?

He'd spent most of his adult life running from emotional commitment because he didn't want to feel the pain of abandonment again. Still, he had to see the child he and Tessa had created, and be a father even though he had no example to work from. William Crawford would never have won a father of the year award.

Inside the room he heard Jordan cough.

This was crazy. Could he deal with her sickness?

Yes. He had no choice. He'd been given an opportunity. Somehow he knew this was where he was supposed to be, except it would be better if Elizabeth were here.

He should leave.

In a few minutes.

Once he took a peek.

No interaction. Just one tiny glance to see what she looked like, then wait for Elizabeth to call. Which she would once she found out he'd been up to the fourth floor.

Do it. He commanded his body. He'd pretend he'd walked into the wrong room, see her and leave.

A bead of moisture meandered down Blake's cheek as he remained plastered against the wall. The rapid sound of footsteps caught his attention.

"What do you think you're doing?" Elizabeth asked.

His plan worked. "I came to see my daughter."

"How did you manage to convince Dr. Stevens to get you in?"

"Eric and I go way back. If it makes you feel any better, he was against the whole idea."

"At least someone had sense. I need to ask you to leave." A chill descended around them.

"I've waited days without a word from you. I'm not going away, Elizabeth. Not until I meet her. I'm her father, I think I have that right."

"You have no rights. The adoption was legal." But the hesitation and doubt in her eyes told another story.

"We'll see about that."

He watched the color drain from her cheeks. The invincible Dr. Randall had disappeared, leaving behind the mother of a sick child struggling for control. Instinctively, he reached out to make sure she didn't fall down. The cool, crispness of her lab coat contrasted the warmth permeating from her skin.

"Is that a threat, Blake?" she whispered harshly as panic twisted her features. Her gaze darted from him to Jordan's room.

He felt like a cad, but he had no choice. "It's a promise."

When she turned to step away, he put his hand out again. His gaze traveled slowly over her as if he were memorizing her in detail. Keeping his voice low, he ground out the words. "Don't shut me out, Elizabeth. Please."

"You can't meet her. Not now. Not yet."

"Why not? Doesn't she know she's adopted?"

Defeat flickered across her face. "No."

The knowledge sucker punched him in the gut. "I don't understand. Tessa—the letter—"

"There's so much you don't know, but I don't feel comfortable talking about it here."

"Then where would you suggest we go?"

The awareness that his hand lingered on her arm made it difficult for her to breathe or come up with anything to say. All she knew was that she felt inadequate and unworthy of the gift God had given her when the obstetrician placed Jordan in her arms, especially now.

Elizabeth felt the weight of everyone's stares on the fourth floor even though she knew it to be a figment of her imagination. The kids on the floor would be oblivious to them, and their parents too occupied to care. The staff might notice Blake, who was sure to set the hospital gossip mill into action, but there was nothing she could do about it now.

Inhaling sharply, she held her breath for a few moments to calm the storm raging inside her. She'd get through this as she had every other uncomfortable incident in her life—by sheer force. She gave Blake a fractured smile and found her voice. "We'll go to the staff break room. This way."

Once inside the small room, her gaze swept over the hands that knew how to cradle, knew how to comfort, knew how to help. Would they help his daughter? Or was this just an act before he decided to rip Jordan from the only home she'd ever known?

What if he tried to contest the adoption? What if he actually sued for custody? Fear and anguish shredded her composure. Why had her attorney suddenly decided to take an extended vacation? She needed to get Arturo's phone number from Marcella.

Elizabeth sank down into one of the plastic chairs. "So, where should I start?"

"How about at the part where Jordan doesn't know she's adopted? Who made that decision?"

"Tessa. She never told me why, but she was adamant. Even though she remained a part of Jordan's life until the end, she was always Auntie Tessa. Even after she died, I kept my promise. Jordan can't find out. I mean, how would you feel if you found out your whole life was a lie? That the mom raising you—" Elizabeth clenched her hands into fists. "I have to protect her. At any cost."

Blake acknowledged her words but remained silent.

Elizabeth reached for his hand. His warmth permeated her skin and an unexplainable energy passed between them. "Please. If you have any feelings for your daughter, you won't challenge me on this. I'll find a way to tell her. Soon."

Elizabeth was grateful Blake blinked, breaking the

connection. He extracted his hand and rubbed it across his face. "I can't believe I'm going along with this."

"Thank you."

"I'm not doing it for you. Now tell me about Jordan."

Inhaling sharply, Elizabeth breathed in the clean scent of soap underneath Blake's aftershave. She turned away from his probing eyes and ran her fingers up and down her stethoscope. "Why don't you tell me what you know and I'll fill in the blanks."

"You adopted Jordan at birth. She doesn't know that she's adopted. Her birth mother was my ex-wife and she has leukemia. For someone who's been alive for almost ten years, that's not a lot."

Elizabeth nodded. There was so much to tell, but they only had minutes because her break was almost over. "Her birthday is May 8. She loves animals, cats especially, and wants to be a vet when she grows up." Elizabeth's voice hitched. *Would* Jordan grow up? "She's normally a fun-loving, active girl, who plays soccer and volleyball."

"If she needs a bone marrow transplant, I want to be tested to see if I'm compatible."

His generosity moved her and time stood still as her gaze traveled over Blake's face, settling on his crystal blue eyes.

Sometimes family members were a match. Some of the time.

"But—"

"Don't try to talk me out of it. You got tested, didn't you?"

"Of course I did, but—"

"I have to do something." At the desperate look in his eyes, Elizabeth kept her thoughts to herself. She'd tested because she wasn't biologically related to her daughter. He'd find out soon enough the odds were against him, no matter that she would pray for a positive match.

"Then, thanks. I appreciate it, because this time around, she needs a bone marrow transplant."

Elizabeth bit down on her lip. "When she got leukemia the first time when she was eight, we got it into remission. It came back right after the new year before Tessa died. She's not responding to chemo this time. She needs to be healthy to get a bone marrow transplant but she's already had three infections. Each one has made her weaker, which is why I can't tell her about you. It would be detrimental to her precarious health. I can't lose her. I won't—not without a fight."

Elizabeth fought hard to keep her tears at bay—losing it in the hospital wasn't an option. But a tear slipped from her eye, and once that one managed to break free, another followed. Within seconds, Blake was by her side, pulling her from her seat, gathering her in his arms.

"We'll get through this, Elizabeth. We'll find a match," Blake murmured as he held her gently. His shirt bunched under her fingers as she freed the emotions that had built up since she'd first gotten Jordan's diagnosis. It felt good, as if she were purging herself. Hope flared deep inside her as he continued to hold her until she had no more tears to cry.

She needed his optimism.

Lifting her head, she stared at him as his thumbs

brushed the moisture from her cheeks. She pulled away from him, reaching for a napkin to wipe the remaining tears. "Thanks, Blake. I—don't normally break down like that."

"Don't worry, your reputation is safe with me."

"As yours is, too." She gave him a hesitant smile. His actions spoke of a caring person, one who could have a positive influence in Jordan's life. Someone who could help her get through each day with support and companionship.

Yet Elizabeth stood there afraid, knowing she couldn't postpone the inevitable. Blake would meet his child, with or without her, as she'd just seen earlier, but it would be better on her terms. "I'll introduce you to Jordan as an old friend. Just until I can tell her the truth, okay?"

"Fine. After all this time, a few more days aren't going to matter. I don't want anything to affect her health either." Blake stepped away, which helped the confusion lingering in the recesses of her brain.

"Thanks, Blake." Hope and wonderment filled her expression as she reached for his hand and squeezed it gently. "Okay, let's go."

As they walked down the hall toward Jordan's room, Blake prepared himself. Most fathers had months to adjust to the idea of fatherhood, not days. Still, he couldn't wait to take a healthy Jordan to the zoo or the bowling alley, or even one of those girly-girl places. Even if they did something as simple as a picnic in the park, he could do the things he'd missed out after his mother died, but with his own child.

"Here we are." Outside room 403 again, Elizabeth turned to face him.

"Here we are," Blake whispered. With his free hand, he pulled at his shirt collar. He stared into her eyes— light blue with flecks of gray. Yet in their depths, he saw a blaze of hope.

Fighting for breath, Blake faced the stark reality of his lonely existence, a reality that could change when he stepped inside the room. She gave him an encouraging smile. "I'll go inside first. Please wait out here."

Before he could stop her, she stepped over the threshold of Jordan's room.

"Hi, sweetheart." Elizabeth was amazed her voice didn't tremble as she approached Jordan's bed. Her daughter greeted her with a smile that lit Elizabeth's world.

"Hi, Mom. What are you doing here? Are you done with your shift already?"

"Well, not yet, but Dr. Jim told me you were feeling better, so I just had to come and see for myself." Sitting on the edge of her daughter's bed, Elizabeth placed her hand on Jordan's forehead, relieved to find it cool and dry.

"Cool. How long can you stay? The Boston Brothers will be right back on. They're singing a new song today."

"The Boston Brothers? Hmm. Have I heard of them?" Teasing Jordan, Elizabeth tucked a thin strand of hair behind her daughter's ear.

"Mom, they're only the hugest, cutest band on the

planet. They're coming to Phoenix, you know. I just saw the commercial." Wistfulness filled Jordan's eyes.

Elizabeth knew her daughter wanted to go to the concert but going to a place with thousands of screaming fans wouldn't be good. A normal immune system could fight off all the bacteria and viruses, but a compromised one only invited them to set up shop, which would delay Jordan's treatment even more.

"We'll see, sweetheart. I can't make any promises, okay?" Elizabeth watched the light fade from Jordan's eyes and wished there was something she could do. Even if her daughter were healthy, tickets had probably sold out months ago. "Maybe next time." Elizabeth squeezed her daughter's hand. "Jordan, there's someone I'd like you to meet. Is that okay?"

"He's not going to poke me or stick me with needles, is he?" Jordan's bottom lip trembled and tears filled her eyes.

Her child had been through so much, and they had so much more to get through to beat the leukemia. Elizabeth forced a smile.

"No. He just wants to say hi."

"Sure. As long as he does it before Tyler, Justin and Shane start singing."

"I'll see what I can do." Elizabeth pushed herself from the bed and went back for Blake. "Okay, are you ready?"

When Blake nodded, she wove her arm through his and guided him into his daughter's room. Silence between the three permeated the small area, broken only by the commercial running in the background. Beside her, Blake stiffened.

Inner turmoil made speaking difficult as her daughter eyed them quizzically. Despite the air-conditioning, the room grew warm. She'd love to take off her lab coat, but without it, she'd feel even more vulnerable and exposed. She inhaled sharply and spoke before she lost her nerve. "Jordan, I'd like you to meet...my friend, Blake Crawford."

"Friend?" Jordan shifted in the bed, careful not to upset her IV. Her eyes widened as she stared at Blake and grinned. "Are you going to get married?"

"Married?" They both spoke at the same time.

Releasing his arm, Elizabeth inched away, her heart thumping furiously inside her chest. Jordan must have gotten the wrong impression. Tom had been the love of Elizabeth's life, but he'd died almost six years ago when Jordan was four—her daughter didn't remember him. She didn't know who wore the more dazed expression, but she felt Blake's almost immediate withdrawal.

Jordan's smile added more tension inside the room. "I saw it on *The Miriam and Teddy Show.* When one of the parents introduces a *friend,* that means they're getting married. Plus, I've been asking God for a new daddy. He *is* good."

Everything had backfired. She couldn't tell her daughter the truth about the adoption, or that her real father stood a few feet away from her. Not yet. Not until they beat the leukemia.

Elizabeth sat on the edge of Jordan's bed and pushed what was left of her daughter's long bangs from her eyes. Now she knew why Blake's were so familiar. There was no mistaking that Jordan was his. She looked back over her shoulder, but he deftly avoided her gaze.

"In this case, Jordan, Blake is just an old friend. He's come to see if he's a bone marrow match, just like all my other friends who are being tested."

Jordan crossed her arms, her lips curving down, disappointment on her face. "That's all? Well, I don't see why you can't get married. I want you to be happy."

"But I am happy."

"Then why do you still cry when you see Dad's picture? People only cry when they're sad."

"That's not true. People also cry when they're happy. Like at weddings and such."

"My point exactly."

When Jordan stuck out her bottom lip, Blake's heart skipped a beat. Tessa used to do that, and it had driven him nuts because he couldn't resist and he'd always given in. But Tessa was gone now, leaving him only with memories and a daughter who was definitely his. A daughter he was afraid to love and possibly lose. The image of another hospital bed rose in his mind's eye.

Forcing his memories back, he let his gaze skim over the doctor again as she sat on Jordan's bed, patting her daughter's hand. In that moment, Dr. Randall disappeared, leaving behind a caring, warm and beautiful woman. It scared Blake worse than running into a burning building without his protective gear.

Elizabeth tweaked her daughter's nose. "We can't get married because we don't love each other."

Relief coursed through him when Elizabeth didn't

encourage this conversation. Yet he found himself wanting to know more about her. Not good. This is how it had started with Tessa when he'd literally run into her outside biology class. That had ended up with a date. And from there, a whirlwind courtship and marriage, which resulted in his daughter's birth. The same daughter who wanted him to do it all over again.

"So why don't you learn how to love each other?"

A strangled cough forced its way out of Blake's lungs over the sound of some boy band. Music. A much-needed distraction right now. He'd eavesdropped on their conversation and knew they'd been discussing this group. "Isn't that The Boston Boys playing?"

"The Boston Brothers," she corrected. But his daughter had a one-track mind right now. "So why don't you go out on dates, fall in love and then get married?"

"Because it doesn't work that way." Elizabeth rushed the words out as she rubbed her daughter's hand again.

"Maybe God isn't real after all." Tears welled in Jordan's eyes.

This conversation wasn't going according to the plan. Blake forced himself to cross the room and stood on the opposite side of Elizabeth, trying to formulate some sort of response. Dread pounded in his heart as he stared down at Jordan and saw the look he'd worn too many times growing up reflected in her blue eyes that were so much like his own. She missed her dad. He'd lost his mom at a young age, at a time when he'd really needed her.

He wanted to tell Jordan the truth, but now that he'd met her, he realized Elizabeth was right. In this fragile state, his daughter probably couldn't handle the news of the adoption.

But something monumental shifted inside him. Blake had been given a chance to come into his daughter's life from this point forward, even if he couldn't tell her the truth. He thrust his fears of blowing it aside as an old saying of his mother echoed in his head. He didn't really believe in the words, but Elizabeth looked as if she needed some help.

"Sometimes God answers prayers in His own time, not yours."

"Well, He'd still better hurry up." Jordan coughed, and concern flashed across Elizabeth's face. There was so much he didn't know about his daughter's leukemia, but he planned to find out.

His gaze met Elizabeth's and he found himself lost in the depths of her blue eyes. Breaking his gaze away, Blake picked up his daughter's other hand. Unfamiliar emotions bombarded him as he held her small, delicate and cold fingers. He tried to infuse a bit of warmth into them while he stared at the child he and Tessa had created.

"Your mom and I are just friends. Nothing more," he said, trying to make things as clear as possible for her. And for himself.

Another frown formed on Jordan's lips, but her attention wandered past Blake's shoulder to the television on the wall. The Boston Brothers were finishing up their latest hit. The light gone from her eyes, Jordan pulled her hands away and resettled herself in her sheets. "Okay. I just thought it would be cool to be a bridesmaid."

Blake's startled gaze met Elizabeth's stoic one. Her lips creased into a ghost of a smile, yet he sensed her dismay.

"Not only will you be a bridesmaid, sweetie, you'll be a bride."

The forced brightness in her voice told Blake that Elizabeth seemed to have lost hope, too. He fought the urge to wrap his arms around her because it would send the wrong message to Jordan.

Seconds ticked by, sliding toward an uncertain future. From somewhere deep in his brain, a distant memory surfaced and he almost felt the urge to pray. Too bad he didn't believe in God. That had been his mom's thing and look where it had gotten her. He shoved his thoughts back where they belonged. Today was what mattered.

And tomorrow.

And the day after that.

"Pinky promise?" Jordan opened an eye and stared at her mom.

"Pinky promise." Elizabeth tucked her pinky through Jordan's and tugged gently. "Now, Mommy's got to get back downstairs before someone misses me. I'll be back after my shift."

Jordan's gaze shifted back to Blake. A tiny bit of color infused her cheeks now and a shimmer of moisture touched her eyes. Blake wove his finger through hers as he'd seen Elizabeth do. "Pinky promise."

He had no idea if he could keep that promise, but he knew he would die trying. He'd do anything to make Jordan happy.

Chapter Four

"I'm sorry, Blake." Elizabeth finally spoke as the bell dinged, signaling the arrival of the elevator. She stared at the red triangle above the metal doors instead of the man shifting on his feet next to her.

"Sorry for what?"

"That Jordan mistook you as my fiancé. She's been praying for a new daddy. I just never thought she'd be so blunt about it in front of a complete stranger."

He stiffened at her words. "I'm not a complete stranger."

Elizabeth knew he spoke the truth. But how, after all these years, could she admit to her daughter—the one she'd promised Tessa she'd love and protect as her own—that she'd gone along with the lie?

But Jordan was her daughter. She wasn't her own flesh and blood, but that didn't matter. It was Elizabeth who had been up doing the nightly feedings. Elizabeth who took care of Jordan's boo-boos and watched her take her first step. Elizabeth who kissed her goodbye as she rode the bus her first day of school. And Elizabeth who consoled her when Tom passed away.

The only father Jordan had known, yet hardly remembered.

She had the power to make her daughter's prayers come true but fear kept her in its grip. What if Jordan chose to go live with Blake when she found out the truth?

"You can't keep her in the dark forever."

She dragged air into her lungs. Words jumbled around inside her head, but no sound passed her lips.

"Look, contrary to what I said upstairs, I won't take her away from you. I just said that to get your attention. You're her mother. You always will be. And I will always be her dad. I'll have to be a bit more patient, that's all. Not one of my strong points."

"Jordan's, either." Her lips cracked into a grimace. "Still, she's been watching too much of *The Miriam and Teddy Show.* Too much TV in general." The doors slid open and Connor Stalling's parents hurried past them. From the concern on their faces, something must have happened with Connor's kidney transplant. Her heart went out to them and she wished there was something else she could do besides pray for his recovery.

"It's not like she has a choice."

Elizabeth watched him push the first-floor button. The interior of the elevator grew smaller and she stepped away to increase the distance between them. "I suppose you're right. She's read almost every book I've brought her and those in the play area, and on better days, she goes and plays games, but still..."

"Maybe me and some of the guys will come in on our days off and keep her company."

"That will help." She paused for a few seconds. "And give you a real chance to get to know her." As she glanced over and saw understanding in his eyes, her stomach lurched. She'd been on this elevator too many times for it to be from the quick descent. The doors slid open and they stepped out onto the tiled foyer. She hesitated, looking between Blake and the empty space behind him. The E.R. was to their right, the entrance to the hospital to their left. Work beckoned, but suddenly she wanted some more time with Blake.

Gently he cupped her chin and tilted her head so she had no choice but to look at him. His nearness brought a measure of comfort and something else she was afraid to identify. "She will get better, Elizabeth."

"From your lips to God's ears." She gathered strength from him, unsure though if there was any truth to Blake's words. God was in control, and she had to believe that Jordan's real father was brought into their lives for a reason.

Blake released her and stepped way, unease rolling off him in waves. "When are you going to figure out God is a figment of everyone's imagination?"

"What?" Elizabeth stared at Blake, their gazes entangled into a thin thread that unwillingly bound them together. "But what you told Jordan—you don't believe?"

Blake leaned against the wall, folded his arms across his chest and stared at her intently. "No, I don't. I'm surprised you do—all doctors believe they *are* God."

"Where did you get that idea?"

Blake scowled. "I have my reasons."

Stunned at the chill in his voice, her heart went out to the man. What had happened that made him feel this way? Even though she hadn't attended church lately, Elizabeth felt God's love surround and comfort her. God had a plan, and no matter what Blake thought, he was involved in it.

"I'm sorry you feel that way." Elizabeth retreated behind the wall of self-protection that served her well in the emergency room setting. "So what do you believe in?"

"Myself."

His flippant answer shocked her. "That's pretty self-serving."

"If you knew how I was raised, you'd understand." Behind Blake's words she sensed his anger, which didn't add up with what she'd come to know about him.

"So when can I speak to Jordan's doctor? I'm assuming just our daughter is to be kept in the dark?"

"Yes. He probably won't be able to meet with us until Monday though."

"That's over two days from now."

Elizabeth heard the sound of approaching sirens and her adrenaline jump-started. She had to get back on the floor. "I can answer most of your questions and concerns, Blake, as well as anything else you'd like to know about—" the unfamiliar words stuck in her throat before she managed to force them out "—your daughter."

"Tonight?"

"I'm sorry. I can't." Elizabeth had already made plans for dinner and a movie with Susie in an attempt to make her life feel more normal. At least that's what her friend had convinced her of anyway.

"Tomorrow night, then?" More angst twisted his features, causing another emotional shift inside Elizabeth.

Her pager beeped. She extricated herself gently. "I need to go. Your friend's father, Dr. Stevens, is retiring tomorrow night. I'm attending his party."

"I am, too. I'll see you there. Maybe we'll find time to talk."

Elizabeth wasn't sure about how she felt about that as she escaped to the E.R. Too much had been thrown at her the last few days and she didn't need another complication in her life. But whether she wanted to acknowledge it or not, it had felt good to have someone else to share her burden with. And that scared her almost as much as the possibility of losing Jordan.

Blake took a deep breath, fingered the few coins in the pocket of his tailored dress slacks and eyed the entrance to the banquet hall at the Camelback Country Club. Missing his protective gear, he fought off the urge to tug at his restricting collar and loosen his tie as he stepped inside the packed room in a suit he hadn't worn since last year. He didn't really belong here among the hospital staff. Why had he come, then? To support his friend's father, and see Elizabeth. He wanted to learn more about her, outside the realm of her work or in relation to Jordan. If they were going to be spending a lot of time together, he figured he should get to know her, to satisfy his curiosity and figure out how to create a unified approach to curing their daughter. Nothing more. He'd learned his lesson about relationships with Tessa.

His gaze surveyed the room again, looking for Eric, his father, the guest of honor and especially Elizabeth. He found Dr. Stevens by the drink station surrounded by a group of people, and Eric engaged in a conversation with an Asian woman still dressed in scrubs. The nurse he was interested in? A grin sprung to his lips. Good for Eric. Just because Blake didn't want to fall back into matrimony, it didn't mean his friend shouldn't take the plunge.

He kept looking around the room, his search for Elizabeth coming up empty. He wondered if she'd ditched the occasion because she knew he'd be here, but as a staff member, he knew her presence was expected.

"Blake Crawford, so good to see you again. What brings you back to our neck of the woods?" Dr. Linden Hall, one of the current hospital board members, clasped him on the shoulder.

"Dr. Stevens, of course." Blake eyed the elderly man with the white tufts of hair for eyebrows, surprised he hadn't fully planted himself in retirement yet. Dr. Hall had to be in his late seventies by now, and should be fishing for trout, not involved in hospital business. Yet some people found it hard to let go of things. Blake should know.

"What are you up to these days?"

"I work for the Phoenix Fire Department."

"As a paramedic?"

"Fireman and EMT."

The old man shook his head. "You're wasting your

talents. Ever thought of going back to school to become a paramedic? I think the city pays for that, doesn't it?"

"They do, and I've thought about it." But not for long, Blake didn't want to fill his hours reading textbooks in school for another 900 hours of training so he could do what a doctor does, but in the field capacity. He enjoyed doing the basic stuff—though he'd picked up some knowledge from his coworkers—and leaving the rest to the professionals like Elizabeth. It was a great way to earn a paycheck and get his adrenaline rush to boot.

Dr. Hall's next sentence went unheard. Blake didn't need to see Elizabeth to know she'd entered the room. He could sense the change in the atmosphere as she stood only a few feet away from him near the entrance. He angled his head to get a glimpse at her, unprepared to see her in a black dress and slight heels.

Stunning was the only word that came to his mind as she clutched her black sequined bag. Normally covered in a lab coat, he'd never had the opportunity to see her in anything else. A hint of blush accented her high cheekbones, and a touch of blue brightened her eyes. And yet, he detected vulnerability he wouldn't normally associate with the doctor. When she glanced around the room, their gazes met and relief flared in her eyes. A slight smile pulled at her lightly glossed lips as she approached.

"Well, good seeing you again. Don't be a stranger at Kingfisher." As if sensing his distraction, Dr. Hall shook Blake's hand before he disappeared, swallowed up by the crowd.

"Dr. Randall, glad you could make it." Before Blake could say a word, a man towing a young blonde around intercepted her as she approached him. "This is Sydney. She's new in Radiology. Sydney, this is Dr. Elizabeth Randall. She's in the E.R."

"Hi, Dale, Sydney." Elizabeth shook the woman's hand, yet she seemed to keep him in her peripheral view. "Pleased to meet you. Welcome to the staff."

"Thanks." Sydney eyed Elizabeth with pity. "Aren't you Jordan Randall's mother?"

"Yes."

"I'm sorry her treatment's not working this time around. I do hope you find a match soon."

"So do I." Blake broke into the conversation. He reached out his hand to the man first. "Hi, I'm Blake Crawford."

"And which department are you in?" Sydney looked him over and he recognized the predatory type instantly. Before he realized what he was doing, he moved closer to Elizabeth.

"He doesn't work at Kingfisher." Elizabeth hesitated slightly. "He's a friend of both mine and the younger Dr. Stevens."

He'd hoped she'd have introduced him differently, but he understood that Jordan needed to know before anyone else. Gossip spread through hospitals faster than a staph infection.

"Then perhaps I'll be seeing a lot of you around, then."

"Nice to meet you," he said as he led Elizabeth away by the arm. "Thirsty?" he asked.

"Yes. Please."

He guided her to the banquet table loaded with drinks. The touch of her warm skin accelerated his heartbeat. He knew he shouldn't feel anything for his daughter's adoptive mother. Learning to be a good father should be the only thing on his agenda, he reminded himself.

"Water? Iced tea?"

"Coffee, actually. I'm a little tired. These type of functions wear me out."

"Really? I'd think you'd love this sort of thing."

"No, crowds make me uncomfortable. But if Jordan were here, she'd be in the middle of the action, not hanging out here by the refreshment table."

Blake sighed as he remembered trying to keep up with all of Tessa's social arrangements. That was another reason he hadn't done so well in school. "Tessa was the same way."

"I remember. I can't believe she even made it through her first semester in med school. I hardly ever saw her, except when she needed some tutoring. I wonder why I never met you, though."

"Because she didn't want anyone to know about me or our marriage for fear it would get back to her parents—wait a minute." His eyebrows rose and his mouth dropped open. "You were her elusive roommate, Lizzy Fairchild? It all makes sense now. She always spoke highly of you even though she didn't understand half the things you said. She trusted you."

That was partially true. Almost a year after she'd dropped out of school, Tessa had trusted Elizabeth enough to let her take and raise her child as her own. But not enough to tell her the name of Jordan's father, who had every right now to claim his position. She fought the wave of guilt and answered Blake's question.

"Was. I changed my last name when I married Tom. As for being elusive, I was always in the library studying because Tessa liked to play her radio a lot."

"She did. I take it you didn't like her kind of music? Here." Blake handed her the cup of coffee and his touch brought a familiarity to the situation that Elizabeth didn't want. He had a charisma about him—she understood why her old roommate had fallen for him.

"It wasn't that. I needed absolute quiet to concentrate." Studying him as he poured himself a glass of water, she took in his just-from-the-barber cut. She missed the slight five o'clock shadow he usually wore, though she had to admit the clean-shaven look was nice, too. Her gaze dipped. Dressed in a suit, he was even better looking than before, if that was possible. But he shifted from foot to foot as his gaze darted around the room. "So tell me, Blake, why are you really here? You don't look comfortable."

"I came to see Dr. Stevens, but I also came to see you. Because we're going to be working together making sure Jordan gets well by supporting her and keeping her spirits up, I thought it might be a good idea to get to know you in more of a social setting."

Elizabeth almost choked on her coffee. Outside of finding a cure for Jordan's leukemia. She'd assumed Blake would want contact only with his daughter—she couldn't handle anything else. Plus, in the back of her mind, she still wondered if he wanted to take Jordan away from her.

Elizabeth needed to put another call in to her attorney. She looked around the crowded room—the sooner she gave her well wishes to the retiring doctor, the sooner she could retreat back to the hospital and Jordan. "There's the doctor. Shall we?"

The distance between them and Dr. Stevens stretched out like a minefield of unspoken thoughts. Out of the corner of her eye Elizabeth let her gaze skim his angular profile and she realized that despite her heels, Blake still stood an inch taller, making her feel protected and secure. Something she hadn't felt since Tom passed away. She couldn't help but acknowledge the strange pull of attraction that flared, and butterflies took hold in her stomach.

"Blake, thanks for coming tonight. I haven't seen you since—" Dr. Stevens grasped Blake's shoulders and stared at him before engulfing him in a bear hug. A genuine smile split the older man's round face.

"My father's funeral. I know."

Dr. Stevens patted Blake on the back. "And who have you brought with you tonight?" As the balding man looked at her, his eyebrows rose and a flicker of concern flashed across his features. "Dr. Randall? Thanks for coming."

His sudden change of expression confused her. She'd worked with Dr. Stevens on occasion when his expertise was needed in the E.R. They were coworkers, yet her presence seemed to surprise him. She glanced in Blake's direction and saw him shake his head slightly at Dr. Stevens. "Sorry to see you go, Dr. Stevens. All the best to you," she said.

"Thank you."

An awkward silence stretched between them as the other doctor continued to shift his gaze between them. A few moments later, another staff member claimed the retiring doctor's attention.

"It's too early to bail. Shall we go get something to eat?" Blake asked.

"I suppose. I haven't eaten since breakfast and it would look pretty bad to leave so soon." Especially if people saw them leave together. Besides, she had to find out why Dr. Stevens and Blake had acted so strangely.

Blake led her across the tile floor. Sidestepping a waiter carrying an empty tray covered with a white napkin, Elizabeth found herself next to an overloaded appetizer table. Her stomach growled as she grabbed a small plate.

"Would you care for some bruschetta?" Blake asked.

"Yes, please. Thanks." Elizabeth hesitated before she held out her plate. It had been years since anyone had seen to her needs. Since Tom. The gesture melted a bit of her reserve.

A few moments later they headed toward the row of tables set up around the exterior of the room. Once seated on the cushioned banquet chair, Elizabeth felt Blake's hand graze the bare skin of her upper back as he helped push her chair in.

The background noise ceased to exist as she struggled with the sensation of Blake's trouch and the effect it was suddenly having on her ability to think. Elizabeth forced herself to forge ahead with her question.

"What was that look for between you and Dr. Stevens?" Elizabeth tucked her napkin on her lap. "What are you trying to hide?"

Blake sat up straight as if distancing himself from her. "I'm not trying to hide anything."

"Then tell me why he was surprised to see us together."

She saw the planes of Blake's cheeks harden and his lips grow taut. His blue eyes turned to stone. "It has to do with your late husband."

Elizabeth set her appetizer down and wiped her fingers on her napkin, mentally going through all the angles in her brain, but came up empty. "Tom was a cardiac surgeon. Dr. Stevens was a neurosurgeon. I don't get the connection."

Blake rolled a grape between his fingers and stared at it intently before he popped it into his mouth. Elizabeth stared at the strong column of his neck before her gaze dropped to watch his fingers tear at his napkin. "My father mentored your husband."

Surprise filled her. "Dr. Crawford was your father? You're the estranged son who had caused him so much grief?" The man sitting next to her bore no resemblance to the son Dr. Crawford had told them about. That man had been irresponsible, self-centered and indifferent. Maybe that was true back then. Maybe even true when he'd been married to Tessa, which could explain why she'd chosen to give Jordan up instead of facing her parents, but not now. Blake cared, or he wouldn't be here.

"Caused *him* grief? He demanded I follow in his footsteps. I didn't want to be a heart surgeon. He disowned me after I dropped out of med school. My father treated Tom like a son instead of me and Dr. Stevens had issues with that. He was more of a father to me than William Crawford ever was. Does that surprise you?"

Her gaze took in the lightly tanned skin, the deep laugh lines framing his eyes and mouth. Now that she sat inches from him, she could see the resemblance to the late Dr. Crawford in the color of his eyes. "Yes, I'm surprised. I never saw that side of your father."

"Not very many people did." Bitterness hardened the planes of his face. Blake's nostrils flared as he inhaled and Elizabeth watched a shutter close over his eyes. "He might have been a great doctor, but he was a lousy father. Which is why I need your help in figuring out how to be a good one to Jordan."

Her heart went out to him. "I'm sorry to hear about your father. Sometimes parents' expectations can be difficult." Elizabeth placed her hand on his and felt a current between them that suddenly made it hard for her to breathe.

"You make it sound like you understand."

"I do," she said, enjoying the feel of his hand a little too much. "I was a child prodigy raised by elderly parents fresh from the old country where one's career was established at the age of five."

"Your parents wanted you to become a doctor, too? What did you really want to do?"

Elizabeth sat still for a moment. "Be a doctor. It had been instilled in me for so long, I wasn't allowed to have any other dreams. My parents were so adamant, their choices became mine. I'm making sure I allow Jordan to choose for herself, though."

"I'm glad to hear that."

Precious moments ticked by, yet neither of them spoke a word. The years slipped backward and she was that gangly twenty-year-old again with no ability to speak to a man who interested her. It had been so easy with Tom. He'd been fifteen years older and a family friend. Gentle and unassuming. A life cut short by a car accident. Tessa's, as well. Would her daughter suffer the same fate but by a different means? A sob worked its way into her throat, making it impossible to swallow, much less talk.

She pulled her hand from his and wrapped it around the ceramic cup, hoping the warmth of the liquid inside would chase away the chill in her veins.

Blake pulled at the collar of his shirt. "It's getting stuffy in here. Would you like to step outside for a moment? I understand the view from here is incredible."

Elizabeth blinked. "I've heard that, too."

A few moments later, the night air slipped around her, the cool temperatures a nice change from the heat of the day. Blake guided her outside, his arm around her waist, which was sure to create more gossip at the hospital, but there was nothing she could do about that now. She enjoyed that sense of protection again.

Strolling along the patio, she thought of how she and Tom had loved to sit outside and watch the sun set over the far edges of the valley from their home in north Scottsdale, especially at the end.

Her fingers twisted the simple gold band hanging from the chain around her neck as her gaze swept over the profile of the handsome man standing beside her. Even though most of his features were in shadow, he filled her senses and made her want to linger. Elizabeth gazed out across the expanse of the dark sea of grass carved into the Sonoran desert. Music floated out the open doors along with the buzz of conversations and the scent of freshly watered lawn lingered in the air.

Her spine stiffened as she stopped by the low stone wall separating them from the edges of the resort golf course. What would Tom think if he saw her with another man? He'd told her to move on and get remarried if anything ever happened to him. That was six years ago now.

She'd loved Tom, and it had been unbearably painful to let go at the end. Elizabeth wouldn't put her heart through that again even though loneliness crept in. Friends couldn't fill the void left by the intimacy of marriage, but until Jordan recovered from her leukemia, Elizabeth had only enough energy to tend to her daughter and her job.

So why did her heartbeat accelerate when Blake was around? Why did she find herself attracted to the one man who had the ability to destroy her life if the attorney decided the adoption wasn't legal after all?

Tessa had known who the father was all along. Maybe Marcella was right. Wouldn't Blake have to sign off on it? But that wasn't what really frightened Elizabeth or made her feel guilty. Maybe, just maybe, she'd coerced Tessa a fraction into giving her the daughter she'd always wanted but couldn't have when she'd fed into her roommate's fear of being cut off from her trust fund.

"Let's go back inside. It looks like the party's really getting started." Blake put his hand under her elbow and led her back through the double doors. She seemed reluctant, but Blake figured it was probably more from the stress of Jordan's illness than anything. He'd rather be back at the hospital, too, but the night away should do her good.

Jazz music played in the background as they found seats near the back of the room and watched Dr. Hall take the podium. "Is this thing on?" He tapped the microphone and Elizabeth winced at the noise. Blake hoped that whatever festivities the organizers had decided on didn't last long, or that the speeches wouldn't be long-winded, so they could both escape.

"Good evening, ladies and gentlemen." Dr. Hall's hearty voice boomed from the microphone. "Thanks for coming tonight. As you know, the good Dr. Stevens is retiring from Kingfisher, and I don't know what you're thinking, but I'm thinking it's about time." Laughter filled the space and Blake grinned at her. She surprised him with one of her own as she nodded.

"I'm starting to think I should retire, too, but I don't know what you'd do without me." More laughter and applause followed. "Now, we thought about doing a roast, but figured you wanted to get home sometime before the end of the month, and we thought about speeches, but didn't want you all to get indigestion, so Nurse Phillips and I thought of the perfect thing."

Behind the doctor, a large screen projected a photo of Dr. Stevens standing outside the O.R.—but instead of wearing his lab coat, he'd donned a Hawaiian shirt and a lei, and he held a ukulele. "Since Dr. Stevens is planning on finally getting his Hawaiian vacation, we thought we'd help him get started. We're going to miss you, Dr. Stevens—enjoy your retirement. Now, everyone get to his or her feet. Ms. Annette is going to teach us to hula dance."

Groans replaced the laughter but, used to taking orders, the staff jumped up, Elizabeth included. She glanced down at him and held out her hand. He shook his head. Blake didn't dance. "Oh, yes, you are. If I'm going to make a fool of myself, you can join right along."

Reluctantly Blake rose. He didn't have much choice. Eric and a nurse joined them with extra leis to put around their necks as a woman dressed in traditional luau garb gracefully stepped up to the front.

Blake tried to follow the instructions, but he couldn't move the right way. Even bending his knees didn't help. Elizabeth had much better luck beside him as she caught on to the movements with both her feet and hands. Somehow he could picture her on a beach in Hawaii, and suddenly he wanted to take her there.

Her laughter filled his ears as she pointed her right foot forward and drew it back. She did the same with her left. "This is fun. If only Jordan were here, she'd have a ball."

"She would, and you can teach her the moves tomorrow. You're superb. I just can't move this way. It's unnatural."

Elizabeth laughed again and gazed over at him, her body swaying to the rhythm of the music. "Relax a bit. You're doing fine, Blake."

And somehow he knew it wasn't just the dancing she was talking about.

"Hi, Mom. How was the party?" Jordan's voice drifted across the stillness of the room.

Elizabeth crossed the room and muted the television, her heels clicking against the floor. "Fine. Just fine. I would rather have been here with you, though. How are you feeling?"

"Tired, as usual. You look really pretty. I didn't know you even owned a dress. I like it. Can I have it when I get older?"

"Of course, honey." Elizabeth glanced down at the black dress she'd worn to the retirement party. Her daughter's words brought hope—as long as Jordan believed she would grow up, she could keep fighting.

She pulled the chair up next to the bed, sat down and then wrapped her fingers through Jordan's.

"Were there a lot of people there?"

Elizabeth squeezed gently. "Of course. Dr. Stevens is a well-respected man who did great things. The staff will miss him."

"Was Mr. Blake there?" Jordan teased her.

"As a matter of fact, he was. He's a friend of Dr. Stevens's son."

"Did you talk? Get to know each other? Kiss maybe?" Jordan had a one-track mind. Elizabeth hated to disappoint her daughter, but it was no use allowing her to get her hopes up.

Releasing Jordan's hand, she set it back down on the bed. "No. Like we told you yesterday, we're friends. Nothing more. Okay, time for sleep."

After Elizabeth tucked the blankets around Jordan, she swept a few wisps of hair from her face and leaned over to kiss her forehead. "I love you. Please say your prayers."

"Love you more." Jordan clasped her hands, closed her eyes and started her prayers.

Elizabeth stood and retreated to the doorway. How fragile her daughter looked, and scared and lonely. One eyelid peaked open and shut quickly when Jordan saw her mom still in the room. A wistful smile touched Elizabeth's lips. She stepped out of the room, hidden from view as she leaned against the wall. As expected, Jordan's extra prayer wafted out on the air-conditioned current.

"Oh, and please God, bring me another daddy. Mr. Crawford seems nice enough. I know Mommy said he's just a friend, but make it something more."

Elizabeth clenched her fists as she stared at the tile floor. She had the power to make Jordan's prayer for a father a reality by simply telling her about the adoption, yet she kept the truth from her daughter because her fears paralyzed her.

If she didn't lose Jordan one way, she would another.

Chapter Five

The next morning, Elizabeth stood outside the main entrance to the fire station where Blake worked, the warmth of the sun beating down on her. Considering it was only the first week of April, the elevated temperatures signaled a long, hot summer. After adjusting the heavy bag on her shoulder, she fanned herself to stir the still air around her while she waited for someone to respond to her knock.

While she'd rather be back at the hospital with Jordan, they had things to discuss. Who was she kidding? She *wanted* to see Blake again. Despite her fears, they had to work together to help Jordan get well. But somehow she knew it went deeper than that.

The door opened and air-conditioned air spilled out from the interior. Blake looked just as good as he had last night, even better with the hint of growth on his chin. Elizabeth found it hard to think, much less breathe. Her reaction to the man still startled her and she grasped to utter a simple hello. "Hi, Blake."

"Morning. Thanks for coming on such short notice.

Hopefully it will be a slow day and we can talk without interruption. Come in." Blake held the door open and allowed her to step inside the cool, dim interior. "Let me introduce you around—otherwise we won't get a moment's peace."

Blake's warm breath against her ear made her stomach turn over. He led her over to the right, where a leather couch, a love seat and a recliner were positioned in front of a large-screen TV. Three other firemen sat around watching a baseball game, eating popcorn and drinking soda.

"Guys, this is Elizabeth Randall. Elizabeth, this is Corey, Matt and Stephano."

"Pleased to meet you all." Elizabeth shook each of their proffered hands.

The medium-built Italian-looking fireman held on to her hand a bit longer than necessary before he raised it to his lips and kissed the back of her hand. "Dr. Randall. Good to see you outside the hospital. You look lovely as usual."

Heat filled her cheeks as she stared at the man. Elizabeth racked her brain over where she'd met the fireman before.

"I'm crushed you don't remember. I used to work at the Saguaro Street station. Kingfisher was the closest hospital."

"Of course. Stephano del Marco. Good to see you again, too." How could Elizabeth forget the Don Juan of the entire Phoenix Fire Department? His conquests were legendary at Kingfisher. Her gaze flew to

Blake's. Stephano had tried to pick her up each time he'd dropped a patient off at the hospital.

"Knock it off. She came to see me, Romeo."

"Not sure why, but when you get tired of him, you know where to find me." Stephano winked at her and returned to the couch.

Blake led her into the open kitchen. A wooden table and six matching chairs invited her to sit down and absorb the stillness surrounding her now that they'd left Blake's coworkers in a different room. How different it was here—she appreciated the quiet.

He pushed in her chair, his hand lingering a moment longer than necessary on the cool wood surface. Elizabeth couldn't figure out if that was a good thing or not. She quickly decided the latter. If she'd learned anything from the experience of losing Tom, she'd do well to remember to guard her heart and not get involved with anyone again.

"Coffee? Water? Soda?"

"Water would be great. Thanks." Elizabeth ran her fingertips along the smooth edge of the wood to avoid watching Blake as he retrieved two glasses and filled them with ice and water. She lost the battle and he caught her staring at him as he turned around and brought the glasses to the table. A crooked smile lingered on his lips as he set the glasses down.

Then he pulled out the chair next to her and sank down on the surface as if only too glad to be off his feet. Elizabeth appreciated the gentle way he held his water and drank deeply until he wiped his mouth with the back of his hand.

A lump formed in her throat. Like father like daughter. "They make napkins for that."

Blake shrugged, yet a hint of red filled his cheeks. "I know. But that would require getting one from the counter. It's just water."

"It's just water, or bread crumbs, or isn't that what washing machines are for?" A melancholy smile creased her lips. Elizabeth had lost count over the years of how many of Jordan's shirts were ruined because of stains, yet now she would welcome Jordan using her shirt as a napkin if it meant her daughter was better. Clothes could be replaced.

"Our daughter does that, doesn't she?" Blake took another drink and Elizabeth could see him struggle not to wipe his mouth.

"Yes. No T-shirt is safe, no matter how many napkins I put by her plate."

"Some habits are hard to break." Her gave her a sheepish grin and grabbed a napkin from the counter.

Elizabeth sensed he meant more than just the topic at hand.

"What type of leukemia are we dealing with?" he asked.

"My—no—our—" Elizabeth had better get used to saying that little three-letter word. "Jordan has ALL or acute lymphocytic leukemia. As I'd mentioned before, she had it when she was eight, and we got it into remission. It came back right after Christmas."

Blake rubbed his face. He reached out and pressed his hand over her clasped one on the table. "I'm sorry you've had to deal with this alone."

His touch soothed her and confused her. It should be easy to confide in Blake. He was Jordan's father after all, but during the years after Tom's death, she'd found it hard to lean on anyone or ask for help. Especially now with Jordan's illness. He squeezed gently and traced his thumb over the back of her hand. Elizabeth struggled not to pull her hand away.

"As I told you before, she needs a bone marrow transplant. It's the only way to get the upper hand." Elizabeth stared out the window along the back wall. Sunlight danced on the palm leaves outside, waving in the gentle breeze. In the background she heard the elevated noise of his coworkers booing at some unpopular call by the umpire.

"The only way?"

Elizabeth nodded. "But we haven't been able to come up with any promising matches. We need to find one soon."

"We will, Elizabeth. We will. If I'm not a match, someone out there is." Blake continued to massage her hand. "When did she get sick?"

Elizabeth wished she shared his optimism, and despite the odds, prayed he would be a match. "It came on quickly. The first time when she was eight, I noticed that she was tired all the time. And then she started to bruise easily. When she started running fevers and complained of headaches all the time, I suspected it was more than a common cold."

"As a doctor, you'd recognize the signs earlier, I suppose."

"Being a doctor had little to do with it. Knowing my

daughter was all it took. If you had known her, I have
no doubt you would have picked up on it, too. Here, I
brought you some things to look at." Elizabeth pulled
her bag off the floor and dragged out two thick photo al-
bums. She scooted her chair closer to Blake so she could
explain the contents of the pictures. Mistake. Being near
him brought out feelings best left buried. She inched
backward a fraction as she opened the first album.

"Here's Jordan's hospital picture, taken the day she
was born." Elizabeth stared at the shocking amount
of black hair on top of Jordan's head, and her daughter's red, scrunched-up face and half-open eyes from
the twenty-hour delivery. Elizabeth had been there the
entire time, encouraging and coaching Tessa through
the labor and yet she still hadn't known if Tessa would
actually give up her baby. She'd begun to question her
decision about giving Jordan up.

But when the obstetrician had placed Jordan in Elizabeth's arms and she looked down at the newborn infant,
love had grabbed hold of her and refused to relinquish
its grasp. A baby. Her baby. Her one chance to create
the family she wanted because she and Tom couldn't
have children. She knew that Tessa must have sensed it,
too, because she'd signed the paperwork the next day.
As part of the adoption, though, Elizabeth and Tom had
agreed to let Tessa be involved in Jordan's life, a decision she'd never regretted.

With each turn of a page, months, even a year flew
by, Blake marveling at the changes in his young daughter's appearance. The wonderment in his eyes gave her
hope that everything would work out.

On the next page, though, Elizabeth's stomach dropped to her knees. She inhaled sharply and tried to turn the page before the scene registered in Blake's mind. Three-year-old Jordan sat on Tom's lap wearing a princess dress and crown as she blew out her birthday candles. Dr. Crawford hovered in the background and so did Tessa—it had been one of the many visits he'd made to see Jordan.

Blake's fingers passed over Tessa's face in the picture as if he could reach out and touch her. Then they hovered over his daughter and finally his dad. "That's okay, Elizabeth. I can handle it."

"Your father was a part of Jordan's life, as well. Now that I think about it, he used to get a faraway look in his eyes when he watched her." She reached out and stroked his arm. "He wasn't the same person you described. And he did believe in God at the end. We used to have long discussions about it after Tom died."

Blake took a few moments to digest her words as he stared at the picture of Jordan with his dad. "I may not have gotten along with my father very well, but he did a lot of good things for people. He saved a lot of lives. So did your husband." His hand caught hers and he squeezed it gently. "We can't change the past, only the future. And all we can do is live each day to the fullest and have no regrets. What's done is done."

Blake's words rang true. Guilt ate at her again. Instead of talking Tessa into keeping the child, Elizabeth had played into her fears of her parents' pulling the plug on her trust fund. Elizabeth should have fought harder for her friend; instead she'd sided with her husband.

Now both Tessa and Tom were dead, leaving only her with the knowledge that they hadn't let Tessa back out on her promise. And each time she looked at Blake she had a sad reminder of the other person who'd lost out, as well.

Monday midmorning, tired and a bit out of sorts, Blake opened the door to the clinic inside Kingfisher, where they would perform the initial test for compatibility. He'd been up most of last night at the scene of an overturned van filled with teenagers. Alcohol and overcapacity had played a major role in the fatalities. Miraculously, two girls had survived—barely—but he knew they'd never be the same again.

His heart went out to the grieving family members gathered upstairs in ICU. He'd wished Elizabeth had been there—after a scene like that accident, it would have been nice to talk to someone other than the guys.

He rubbed his hand over his face before he stepped up to the counter to sign in. The girl behind the counter gave him a harried smile before she glanced down. "Hi, Mr. Crawford. Have a seat—we'll call you back shortly."

"Thanks." His gaze swept across the crowded room, finally spotting a vacant chair tucked in the corner. He barely made eye contact with the slender middle-aged man in the seat next to his, wearing a blue button-down shirt and khaki pants. Blake leaned against the wall on his other side and stretched out his long legs.

In the background the television droned, mingling with the sporadic conversations of the people waiting. Blake closed his eyes—this was going to take a while.

"Eight teenagers lost their lives last night in a horrific accident on Loop 101. Two remain fighting for their lives," the usually perky afternoon newscaster reported in a subdued manner. Blake didn't need to hear the rest of the details about the mangled van or see the pictures. He'd lived it firsthand.

"Bad accident." The man next to him spoke.

Blake really didn't want to engage in a conversation with him. He opened his eyes and stared at a dried water spot on the ceiling. Anything to avoid looking at the pictures and listening to the police and witnesses rehashing the scene.

"Such a waste." Out of the corner of his eye, Blake saw the man shake his head. He obviously didn't get that Blake wasn't in the mood for conversation as he continued. "They had their whole lives in front of them."

Just as his daughter was supposed to have her whole life in front of her. "They weren't thinking about that when they consumed all that alcohol and got into that van. Especially the driver. She's going to have to live with that decision the rest of her life."

"Sounds like you were there."

"I was. Blake Crawford. Phoenix Fire Department." He turned and acknowledged the speaker. Wisdom and compassion filled the older man's gentle blue eyes, while an inner peace and strength radiated from within.

Blake wondered what it would take to achieve that sort of calmness as he shook the man's outstretched hand. For such a slight build, his firm grip surprised Blake. "Mark Ferguson. Pastor at Desert Light on Shea."

A pastor. Of course. Blake hadn't thought of God in

years and now in a matter of days, he'd been confronted by him three times. An uncomfortable feeling balled in the pit of his stomach, but he wouldn't read anything into this other than coincidence. "Nice to meet you."

"Likewise. After I finish here, I'm going upstairs to offer support to the Mullen family. Their daughter, Stacy, was the driver. Thanks for your quick thinking and hard work last night. It made a difference."

Making a difference.

On the way back from another call, they were only seconds away from the scene and were the first to arrive. Seconds had made a difference. Blake had never thought about it that way. Being an EMT and a fireman was a job he had fallen into once his enlistment ended and he returned to the Valley. Yet today he felt the weight of how important his job was. Something inside him shifted and a lightness started to push out the darkness that had consumed him from the day he walked into Elizabeth Randall's life.

"I hope she makes it. The other girl, as well," he said.

"That's in God's hands now." Mark clasped his hands and raised his gaze upward for a few seconds. Blake shifted on the now-uncomfortable seat as the pastor asked, "Are you here to donate blood?"

"No. Not a bad idea, though."

"Mark Ferguson?" The petite brunette holding a clipboard announced through the doorway leading to the interior of the clinic. "Please come on back."

Mark rose to his feet and extended his hand. "Nice chatting with you. If you ever need to talk, stop by the church and see me."

"Give my best to Stacy's family." Blake refrained from replying to the pastor's offer. He couldn't imagine why he'd want to talk to the pastor. He'd had enough of that in his youth. It hadn't done any good then; it wouldn't do any good now.

The news commentator came back on, listing all the things to do around Phoenix that weekend. Blake closed his eyes and leaned his head against the wall again. Images from his past flitted through his mind like an old movie reel. Riding the merry-go-round at Encanto Park and then stopping by Mary Coyle's for ice cream. Holding his mom's hand as they walked through the old neighborhood, or hearing her clap and holler at his Little League games. Opening the gifts under the tree on Christmas morning, or the silly hats she made him wear on his birthday. If he'd known the future, he'd have only been too glad to put that paper cone on his head when he'd turned ten, because months later, his mom would be dead.

Pain tore his insides to shreds. He'd shut those memories off years ago. Put them in a place where they couldn't hurt him anymore. And yet now that they'd been released, his attempts to shove them back into the dark recesses of his brain failed. His memories took on a new life.

They were on the beach in San Diego, a family walking hand in hand. More often than not, a six-year-old Blake would dart away and splash through the surf. If he was brave enough, he'd lie on the beach and let the ocean roll over and around his body, the sand coarse and rough against his tender skin. Sometimes his dad would join him and his mom would laugh as she snapped photos. His father had been a different person back then—not as distant, with a ready smile for the love of his life and his son.

Blake realized the light had gone out for both of them when Laura Crawford died. William buried himself in work, as if trying to atone for his failure to heal his wife. In doing so, he'd shut out his son, who'd desperately needed him.

And now Blake had a daughter who needed him, yet he was afraid, afraid of bonding with someone who might disappear just like his mother had.

"Blake Crawford?" the nurse called.

Once inside the small room, he sat and waited, his fingers drumming against the Formica counter. His foot tapped on the floor, courtesy of all the caffeine he'd inhaled to help him stay awake. Medical posters lined the walls, but he barely registered the contents, his focus on the cotton swabs and gloves lying on the counter.

The door opened and a redhead dressed in a cats-and-dogs smock entered. "Hi, I'm Olivia. So you're here for an initial bone marrow donor compatibility test?"

Blake nodded as the young woman sat down in the chair opposite him and reached for a cotton swab.

"Here. Just swab your cheek for me." Olivia handed him the swab. "When you're done put it in the container and that's it."

Blake did as he was told and handed everything back to Olivia. "That's it? I was expecting more. Don't you take blood samples?"

Olivia placed the vial on the counter and swiveled

back to face him. "Not the first time around. What the doctor is going to look for is a matching tissue type."

"HLA."

"Right. If your human leukocyte antigen is a close match to that of the patient, it's better. If that's the case, then you'll be brought back in to give a blood sample or another cheek swab."

"I'm testing for my daughter."

"Your daughter?" The woman stilled and shifted her gaze to a spot behind his shoulder.

"She has leukemia. I'm sure everything will come back positive." Blake stood and scratched the back of his neck, hesitating because the lab tech remained in her chair.

"I'll put a rush on this, then." Sorrow and compassion touched Olivia's features as she stared up at him. "I don't want to bring you down or anything, Blake, but I think you should know that only thirty percent of people are matches for family members."

Chapter Six

Last night's accident still clawing at his emotions, Blake stood outside Jordan's door later that afternoon. Mark and Corey and the others found solace in their families, but Blake knew that unloading on the sick child on the other side of the wall wasn't an option. Elizabeth either.

She had had more of a relationship with his father than he had, and he was actually having a tough time with that.

Clenching and unclenching his fists, he waited, looking for an opportunity to go inside. He wasn't sure why he'd come back today, except he wanted to see Jordan again. Had to see her. Especially since there was a good possibility that he wouldn't be a match. Why hadn't Elizabeth told him? His thoughts charged back to that conversation in the break room. She'd tried, but he'd cut her off. Though deep down he realized that the flicker of emotion that had passed across her face meant she dared to hope he might be the one who could make his daughter well. Maybe he would be in that 30 percent? Though realistically, finding out he was her father would benefit her emotionally.

But until that happened, he had to settle for being Elizabeth's friend. And Jordan's, as well.

A commercial for The Boston Brothers and their up-coming concert leaked out into the hallway, giving him an idea. He knew enough about Jordan's illness now to know that she wouldn't be able to attend the concert because of her compromised immune system, but that didn't mean he couldn't try to make other arrangements.

He knocked on the open door and stuck his head in-side. "Hi, Jordan. May I come in?"

"Mr. Crawford." A smile lit Jordan's lips. A strange emotion caught him off guard as it slipped in past his defenses and tugged at his heart. "Sure. Is my mom with you?"

"No. I was downstairs getting tested for compatibil-ity and thought I'd say hi." He didn't need to have Eliza-beth with him—Jordan was his daughter and he had the right to see her. A little over two weeks had passed since he'd learned of her existence, yet it felt like a lifetime.

He'd done a search online about how to be a good dad and the information that had popped up astounded him. It seemed so easy, yet he was realistic enough to know that words on a screen simplified the enormous task ahead of him. But he could start with the "spend time with them" and "have fun together" part.

"Are you a match?"

"It's too soon to tell." Blake sat in the chair near her bed.

"Hang on. My mom says it's rude to keep the TV on so loud when company visits."

When Jordan lifted her arm to mute the television, Blake saw the IV. How fragile and small she looked in the hospital bed, even though Elizabeth had done her best to make it feel homey with the colored sheets, stuffed animals and a few other personal items from home.

His daughter eyed him speculatively, her large blue eyes taking him in. "Do you have a job? Most people work on Mondays."

Blake nodded. "I work for the City of Phoenix as a fireman and EMT. We have twenty-four-hour shifts and days off in between. I got off work at eight o'clock this morning."

"Oh. What's an EMT?"

"Emergency medical technician. All firemen have that training here in Phoenix. I don't quite get to do all the exciting things a paramedic does, but I do get to drive the ambulance and offer basic aid."

"Cool. Can you take me for a ride on a fire truck sometime?"

At the hope etched into her face, Blake struggled to find the right words. His childhood had been filled with so many disappointments, he didn't want Jordan to experience the same broken promises. Ride-alongs weren't permitted, but he could bring her by the station for a visit. "I think I can arrange something." In the meantime, he channeled the conversation in another direction. "So, what do you want to be when you grow up?"

He knew because Elizabeth had told him, but he wanted to hear it from his daughter's lips.

His daughter.

He would do his best to be a great father to her. And if he wasn't a match, he'd do his best to find someone who was.

"A vet. I love working with animals."

Leaning forward in the chair, Blake rested his elbows against his knees. "Why not be a doctor like your mom?"

A frown creased Jordan's brow. "Because—because—I don't know. It takes up a lot of her time. Sometimes I wish…never mind. She does a lot of good. The Lord's work on earth. I can do it, too, but with animals."

"Yes, you can." It didn't surprise him that Jordan had the same beliefs as her mom, and yet all this talk about God since he'd come into Elizabeth's life made him squirm.

"My mom says that its very hard to get into vet school and that I need to study a lot. I'm not worried, though. My mom's smart, and so was my dad. He was a doctor, too, you know."

Blake didn't dare correct her. "I came by to see if you wanted to play a game or something. It's got to be pretty boring to watch TV all the time."

"It is. How about a game of checkers? It's over there by the window."

"Works for me." Blake stood and retrieved the box from the table. Then he pulled the tray table over Jordan's bed and opened the lid.

"Mr. Crawford, can I call you Mr. Blake instead? It's not quite so formal."

Blake would rather she call him Dad, but that wasn't his call to make. Yet. He dumped the pieces out on the board. "Sure. You can call me Blake if you want to."

"No. That's okay. My mom says that a child using an adult's first name is not respectful. I have to say I agree with that."

Her choice of words amused him. She sounded a lot older than her years. "Red or black?"

"Red, please." With her free arm Jordan quickly placed her pieces on the squares. "Mr. Blake, can I ask you a question?"

"Sure." As she eyed him, Blake got a little nervous.

"None of my mom's other friends come in and play games with me. I get this weird feeling I should know you." Jordan's gaze wandered over Blake's face.

Blake nearly jumped to his feet, but forced himself to stay seated. "There's no way you could know me, Jordan. This is only the second time we've talked. I can't speak for your mom's other friends, but I suspect they have regular jobs. I have a lot more free time. Your mom said that it would be okay if I came to see you on my days off. To keep you company and help you get through this. That's all."

"I wish God would hurry up and grant my prayers. I know my mom's trying to protect me, but I know the truth. She just doesn't want to talk about it."

His heart stalled. "What truth, Jordan?"

"That if we don't find a bone marrow donor, I'll die. I'm not afraid, because I'll be with Jesus and all the other little children that have gone to Him, and I'll be with my dad again, but my mom will be left here. Alone. Which is why I want a new daddy. For my mom."

If only he could tell her the truth. Maybe he should point out to Elizabeth that the knowledge could possibly be the turnaround they needed to keep Jordan from getting so many infections until they found a donor. He stood inches from Jordan, yet the gulf between them stretched out like miles. He wasn't so sure he agreed with Elizabeth's position anymore.

The urge to pick up Jordan's hand and hold it in his overwhelmed him. He had the power to give her part of what she wanted. He could be her father, but loving Elizabeth scared him. He hadn't gotten it right the first time—what made him think he could or even should try again?

"We will find a donor for you, Jordan. As for the rest, you'll just have to keep praying and see what happens."

"Well, it was worth a try, but I'm sorry." Dr. Jim Pearson pulled his glasses from the bridge of his nose Thursday morning and looked away from the pile of papers on his desk. The overhead lights reflected off his cropped white hair and deepened the shadows under his faded blue eyes. As his gaze went between Blake and Elizabeth, the lines bracketing his mouth intensified. "Blake's not a match either."

Even though she knew this would happen, Elizabeth was crushed. Her carefully planned world crumbled beneath her sensible black flats. Her stomach muscles clenched and nausea took hold. Despite the odds, she'd prayed Blake would be a bone marrow match. Elizabeth didn't know how much more pain she could endure.

Her fingers wandered to the stethoscope wrapped around her neck and she ran her forefinger and thumb up and down the flexible tubing. She stared at the bookshelves filled with books behind Jim's head, not believing there wasn't an answer to their daughter's leukemia inside one of them. She stood, unable to remain in the brown leather chair anymore. "Where do we go from here?"

Blake stood with her and in a heartbeat, wrapped his arm around her shoulders. She relished the comfort and strength even for the short time. The agitation consuming her body demanded movement. Action.

Jim stood and walked around his crammed desk and set his hip against the dark cherry-stained wood. "I checked again and the registry turned up two new possibilities. We'll start with those."

"Sounds like a plan." Elizabeth turned away. A quick glance at Blake's colorless features and firm, straight lips told her more than his unsaid words. She walked to the window overlooking the street, where Blake joined her moments later. In the distance she could see children playing in a park and wondered if Jordan would ever do the same again. "What aren't you telling us?"

The doctor sighed and joined them at the window. "Like I said from the start, Jordan has unusual markers. Testing family members was a good idea, I'm sorry it didn't work. Let's focus on an unrelated donor. New ones hit the registry every few days, I'll keep checking. Now, if you'll excuse me, I have to meet someone in the cafeteria. Take all the time you need in here and feel free to call me about anything."

Once the doctor left the room, Elizabeth stared past the glass pane as if looking for an answer. They were running out of time, yet she refused to give up. She couldn't. Because then she'd have to admit defeat and she wasn't willing to do that yet. "Maybe it's time to call Tessa's parents. I think they should probably know they have a granddaughter. Who knows? Maybe one of them might be a match, as unlikely as it seems."

Blake shifted on his feet. "Maybe. Tessa was adopted herself, so there'd be no biological connection."

"Really?"

"Yes. That's why she must have insisted Jordan not know about the adoption. She grew up knowing of her adoption and it bothered her." Blake pressed his fingers to his eyelids, memories bombarding him relentlessly. "Right after our marriage, Tessa had attempted to contact her birth mother with disastrous results." That was when things had changed between them. And yet when Tessa had found herself pregnant, she'd repeated her mother's actions. Bile rose in the back of his throat. "That family wanted nothing to do with her then—they won't care about a daughter of hers, no matter how sick."

"I still have to try. I can't rest until I explore every possibility."

"Then I'll be there when you make the call." He knew it would be a waste of time and that Elizabeth would need him when she hung up the phone. Blake paced the small confines of the room. He didn't like where his thoughts were taking him.

"I'll also organize a bone marrow drive to widen the possibilities," Blake said. "Who knows how many other parents are in the same predicament? Getting more people to register can only help us and them." Blake surprised himself. Since when had he started thinking about others first outside of work? Since he'd met the doctor and his daughter.

He gathered Elizabeth in his arms and stroked the silky softness of her short brown wavy hair. The way she fit against him felt as if she were the missing piece to a puzzle that he had no idea he was searching for. No other woman had ever made him feel this way, even Tessa.

Later that afternoon, Blake rested his hand against the wood door before he pushed it open. Immediate darkness surrounded him until he took off his shades. In a few moments, his sight adjusted to the lighting inside the church office. The matronly woman sitting behind the computer screen looked up and smiled at him. "Hi, welcome. I'm Linda. How may I help you?"

"Blake Crawford." His feet rooted themselves to the floor and he questioned why he was there. He needed to talk to someone, and the pastor was the only person he could think of, but now it seemed like a mistake.

He'd quit believing years ago, although he didn't really worship himself like he'd mentioned to Elizabeth the other day in the hospital when they'd been talking about God. That had been a knee-jerk reaction to hide the hurt that had festered inside him all those years he'd spent in isolation after his mother died. But what use would it be to see the pastor, or the Pope for that matter? If he couldn't help his daughter, what made him think that the God Elizabeth believed in could? "I—I'd like to speak with Mark Ferguson."

"Have a seat, then." Linda picked up the phone and hit a button. "Pastor Mark? There's a Blake Crawford here to see you." The woman tapped a pen against her lips as she listened to the response. "Okay." She hung up. "He's finishing up something on the computer. He'll be out in a minute or two. Feel free to have some coffee while you're waiting."

Too keyed up to sit, Blake forced himself to grab a drink of water from the fountain around the corner. The coldness temporarily relieved his parched tongue. Being inside a church again brought up old anxieties and insecurities, not the relief people he knew talked about.

He shouldn't have come. And yet, he'd felt he had to.

He took another drink yet he couldn't deaden his thirst or his unease. Tension bit into his shoulders and between his eyes as he straightened, his grip still tight on the sides of the metal basin. His brain warred with his feet, trying to convince them not to run out the front door.

While he could escape the building, he couldn't escape the devastating news that he wasn't the answer to his daughter's leukemia. Back to square one with no donor in sight. He didn't need a medical degree, Elizabeth or even Jordan to tell him they were almost out of time.

He turned away from the fountain. The building reminded him of a vee, with the entrance at the bottom and two short hallways branching off from the receptionist's desk. Instinctively, he looked for the exits and working smoke detectors. Sprinklers had been installed in the ceiling. The front door where he entered was behind him and down the hallway to his left, another door was clearly labeled as an exit. Signs above the doors signaled that the meeting rooms, library and children's ministry flanked either side of hallway. The right hallway housed the offices and a counseling area but dead-ended into a wall.

Like his life right now. How could he be a father to Jordan if Elizabeth wouldn't tell her the truth? But how could he insist on that if it could jeopardize her life?

His long strides made short work of the distance to the sofa. He detoured to stare at the pictures gracing the wood end table. Several of them showed the man he'd met at the clinic standing with a group of Native American children in front of an old adobe building.

"We support a church near Kayenta by bringing supplies, medicine and clothing. Hi, Blake. Good to see you again."

Blake turned to see the pastor. He shook his hand. "You, too. Thanks for seeing me."

"No problem. Sorry for the wait." The man's gentle smile put Blake at ease. "This way, my conference room is a bit messy, but it's cleaner than my office." Mark glanced at the woman behind the desk. "Linda, don't wait for us. I'll lock up when I leave."

He led Blake down the hallway and ushered him into

the room on their right. Piles of purses filled one corner and boxes of assorted sundries filled another. As if understanding Blake's curiosity, Mark waved to the piles. "We're repainting the meeting room. Our women's ministry puts together purses for Mother's Day for the less fortunate women in the shelters in South Phoenix."

And all Blake did with his spare time and money was chase after the next thrill. His last excursion of parachuting paled in comparison to the difference these people were making in others' lives. This was the sort of thing his mother would have gotten involved in. And now that he thought about it, even his dad had a philanthropic side and supported his favorite charities.

Blake would start in his own way by coordinating the drive for his daughter and the other people in need.

"Would you like a bottle of water?"

"No, thanks."

Mark ushered him into a seat and took a matching chair to his left.

"So how's Stacy doing?" Blake asked.

"She's out of ICU but still has a long way to go. Thanks for asking." Mark folded his hands together. "So, how can I help you?"

The air-conditioning unit kicked on and a blast of cool air chased away the warmth that had settled around Blake. He shifted on the seat. A light sheen of moisture gathered on his hands as he clasped them together and stared at the swirl pattern on the throw rug beneath his feet. This had been a bad idea.

"I don't know. I don't even believe."

"That's a tough spot to be in. What is your spiritual background, then?"

"My mom believed. We used to go to church when I was a kid. Then she died from breast cancer and we quit going. That's my story." Blake wiped a hand across his face, trying to hold back the memories. Sundays had always been special. While he hadn't liked dressing up in a his Sunday best and uncomfortable shoes, he had liked spending the time with his mom. Afterward, they'd go to breakfast and then out to his grandparents' house, or the park, or somewhere else special. Sometimes his dad would come with them, but most of the time he was working.

"I see. How old were you?"

"Ten."

Mark leaned forward and rested his elbows on his knees, compassion in his eyes. "Losing a parent is never easy, especially when you're young."

"So why did He do it?"

"God doesn't do bad things to us, but He allows things to happen to strengthen us so we can achieve the potential He has in mind for us. Our God is all-loving. He doesn't want us to be sick. Think about the pain she suffered. Would you have wanted her to continue that way?"

Blake clenched his hands again. He wasn't here to talk about his mother and how she suffered as the cancer ravaged her body, making her skinny and weak and unable to even hold him in comfort at the end. Blake dug his fingernails into his thighs. He would not cry. He still wasn't sure why he was here at all.

"Then why didn't He heal her? Jesus healed blind men and lepers and cripples."

"A lot depends on if that person's purpose has been fulfilled. We each are given a certain number of days here. There are more for some than others. Take the accident the other night. Six girls were called home immediately, Stacy and one other remain here. They haven't achieved what God wants them to achieve yet."

A stagnant silence filled the room as Mark gave Blake time to digest his words. "I sense you're still angry with God for taking her from you, and yet you're here, in God's house."

Pent-up energy forced Blake to stand and pace. None of this made sense and he longed to escape to the gym and take out his frustration on the machines. Or better yet, call Eric and shoot a quick game of hoops where their conversation would revolve around basketball or some other equally inane topic. Nothing so deep, so gut-wrenching.

"God's house? All I see is a room in a building."

"That's true. And you might argue that man made the building and everything inside. But look deeper. Where did the knowledge to build this come from? Where did the materials used to construct it come from? Look outside at the trees and cactus and birds. You've got a medical background. You've probably seen inside the human body. Tell me that the wonders around us and inside us are just a coincidence." Blake thought about the pastor's words. "Now you say you don't know why you're here, but I think you do."

Blake nodded. "My daughter has leukemia. I'm not a

match to be a bone marrow donor for her. I don't know where to turn. If we don't find a donor, she'll die."

Mark stood and placed a gentle hand on his shoulder. "I'm sorry to hear about your daughter. I'll keep her in my prayers. How can I help?"

"We want to do a bone marrow drive to widen the pool and need a place that can accommodate us." Blake spurted out the first thing that came to him.

"Why not do it here? We have a few rooms to choose from, depending on the size you think you'll need."

Relief filled him. Maybe that was the reason he'd chosen to come here today. Maybe subconsciously, he was looking for a place big enough to hold the drive. The church fit perfectly. "You'd do that for a non-believer?"

"Despite what you think, we're all God's children. I would do it for you and for the next person walking through my doors. But Blake, is there something else troubling you, as well?"

"I don't know. I feel so alone. Lost. Like I have nowhere to turn."

"Reaching out to God is a start. I can help you with that."

Blake turned his back on the scene beyond the window and the man still standing by it. He began pacing again, the small confines of the room starting to grate on his nerves. "What good would that do? What makes you think He will save the daughter I didn't even know existed until a few weeks ago?"

Pastor Mark walked back to the end table and took a drink from his water bottle. Seconds ticked by as he slowly twisted the lid back on and studied the clear contents before capturing Blake's gaze. "Perhaps this is God's way of bringing you together with your daughter. And because none of us know how much time we have here, I'd suggest you make the most of the time you have together."

Chapter Seven

"Have a moment?"

Blake startled Elizabeth as she exited the E.R. after her shift later that day.

His touch chased away the heaviness that had descended on her brain. While her steps didn't have a sudden spring to them, they didn't exactly clod against the tile as they had a moment earlier.

"Of course, but I need to see Jordan first. When and where should I meet you?"

"It's just after five o'clock now. I'll pick you up here at six-thirty." His statement left her no room for argument, no gray area for her to conveniently forget about their meeting. She knew they had to discuss Jordan's care, especially after the news from Dr. Jim earlier that day. They needed to work together to get Jordan healthy.

Relief touched her heart that she wasn't alone in this right now, yet part of her remained detached. She did not want to get involved with Blake any more than she had to—her heart couldn't take it. "Pick me up?"

"You're probably tired of cafeteria food. I know a

great restaurant not too far from here." His intense gaze made her catch her breath. "I've been busy since I saw you this morning. I haven't been able to contact Tessa's biological mother yet, but I have her adoptive parents' phone number. I doubt you want to talk to them here inside the hospital."

"You're right. I'll meet you outside the front entrance at six-thirty." There was no way she'd go out through the employee door or by the E.R. where a coworker might misconstrue their meeting. She'd heard enough rumors after the retirement party last weekend but had managed to put them to rest. It would be hard to do that again.

Five minutes before Blake's intended arrival, Elizabeth paced by the sliding front doors and the curb, her emotions torn apart. Jordan didn't feel well and her look of disappointment when Elizabeth told her she couldn't stay shredded her composure. Elizabeth should be upstairs, but she also knew she and Blake had to pull together a bone marrow drive to find more people for the registry. Blake had insisted they leave the hospital. Probably a good thing because Elizabeth hadn't seen the sun in days. The warm breezed danced across her skin, a contrast to the air-conditioned temps inside.

Leaning against a stuccoed pillar, Elizabeth crossed her arms and stared across the sea of asphalt to the natural area by the parking lot. Birds fluttered on the ground and in the trees while rogue rabbits munched away at the carefully manicured flower beds. Nature still managed to exist in the city. She inhaled the fresh scent of spring as the hum of evening traffic filled her ears. God's world amazed and left her in awe of His power and goodness.

He had a plan, and she had to go along with it—on His time, not hers.

True to his word, Blake pulled up in a red Jeep at six-thirty and stepped from the vehicle. Elizabeth's heart fluttered when he stopped beside her, his clean, fresh scent tickling her nose and adding another layer of indecision into the mix. "Hi," he said, his appreciative gaze sweeping over her.

Elizabeth made no move toward the vehicle, her feet planted on the cement. Leaving the hospital wasn't a great idea after all. Not when his slow, easy smile made her more aware of him as a man rather than the father of her child. "Jordan's developed another infection at her IV site."

He thrust a hand through his hair in frustration. "She looked fine when I saw her earlier."

"You saw her today?" Elizabeth wondered why no one had told her Blake had gone up today, because they'd informed her of his visits almost every day this week. She searched his blue eyes.

Worry and something else she was afraid to identify surfaced in their depths and stole the air from her lungs. He was falling in love with Jordan.

"Before our meeting with Jim. She was sleeping, so I didn't wake her."

"Because she was getting sick again." Elizabeth broke the contact and stared at the City of Phoenix logo embroidered on his dark gray polo shirt. "Antibiotics will knock the infection out, but every little thing now will set back her road to recovery. If—"

He wrapped his hands around her upper arms and squeezed gently, his intensity giving her strength. "We will locate a compatible donor. I won't rest until we find one." The setting sun cast an orange glow on his features as his jaw hardened a fraction and determination filled every angle of his face. "Change in plans. What's Jordan's favorite thing to eat?"

"She's already had dinner."

"I've eaten hospital food. If our daughter is to get better, she needs the real stuff. So what does she like?"

"Chicken Pad Thai."

"Chicken Pad Thai?" His eyebrows rose and he dropped his hands from her arms. "I expected a quick burger and fries, or chicken fingers."

"You consider that real food? Full of preservatives and fillers? We don't usually eat fast food."

He smiled at her and butterflies took flight in her stomach again. "Chicken Pad Thai it is. What do you like?"

"We usually share, and I get an order of pot stickers."

"Go upstairs to Jordan. I'll be back shortly." Blake strode to his parked Jeep and pulled away, leaving Elizabeth out of sorts.

She was so used to taking care of everything since Tom had gotten sick, the mere idea of someone else taking charge seemed foreign. Blake didn't seem the type to sit around and let others make decisions on his behalf. She had to admit the change felt good. But scary, too. She could no longer deny that she was beginning to care about him.

Some thirty minutes later, Blake came to Jordan's room carrying a white plastic bag and a tablecloth. Elizabeth's stomach growled at the rich, tangy smell of the Thai food. She rose from her seat and pulled the dark-blue-and-white-flowered fabric from his hand.

"A tablecloth?"

"Corey's wife, Karen. I think she's trying to civilize me. I thought it might be a good idea."

Elizabeth had tried to make the place homier, but nothing could hide the fact they were in a hospital. All they could do for Jordan was try to have some fun.

"Ready for your picnic?" Blake said.

Jordan clapped her hands, careful not to upset her IV. "A picnic in my room. Taylor will be so jealous. I can't wait to tell her. When can she come visit?"

"When you get well. Mr. Blake and I have a few things to discuss later, so why don't you call her after dinner and see how she's doing?"

Elizabeth glanced at Blake as he started to set up. He certainly had all the makings of being a good father despite his request for her to help him figure it out.

She helped him drag the side table over next to the bed and tray table to create a bigger eating surface. Then she watched as he unfolded and draped the tablecloth over the tables, his hands gentle as he stroked away the creases. The tip of his tongue protruded from his lips as he worked, and she noticed a tiny scar at the crown of his head. No hair grew on the thin line—with his hair cropped short, she'd missed it until now.

He looked up, their gazes connecting. "Where did you get that scar on your head?"

"Skiing accident in high school. I went off trail. It could've been worse."

"You really should be more careful," Jordan piped in, adjusting herself into a better position to eat.

Blake's gaze strayed to Jordan. "I should, shouldn't I?"

"You should. People who take chances like that always end up in the hospital. At least, that's what my mom says." Jordan's voice held censure and it made Elizabeth squirm. Did she really sound like that? So old and...not fun? Her cheeks heated as she made eye contact with Blake again.

"Your mom has a good point." They continued to stare at each other. Emotion pooled in his eyes and held her spellbound until Elizabeth heard Jordan rearrange the sheets around her legs.

Breaking away first, Elizabeth went to the corner and dragged the chair to the makeshift table. "We'll need to get another one."

"Tell me where to go and I'll get it."

"The break room, down the hall. Do you remember where it is?" Elizabeth focused on pulling out the food from the plastic bag. Her cheeks burned and it was all she could do to make sense of the scribbled writing on the top of the white cartons.

"I do." Even though Blake had escaped the room, Elizabeth could still sense his presence and the lingering scent of his clean aftershave. While the room appeared bigger in his absence, she knew it was just an illusion. The room hadn't changed a bit—just her perception of the man who'd recently vacated it.

"Mom, are you sure you're just friends?"

At her daughter's words, Elizabeth's hand stilled on the last carton before she pulled it out of the bag. Blake's Kung Pao Chicken. "Yes, I'm sure."

"Well, you sure look at each other weird." Expectation filled Jordan's eyes.

Blake returned just in time with another chair. After setting it down on the opposite side of Elizabeth's, he pulled out hers and motioned for her to sit. Then he leaned over and settled a napkin on Jordan's lap before tucking one into his collar.

Jordan's laugh warmed Elizabeth's heart, as did his actions. "You're funny, Mr. Blake. Napkins are supposed to go on your lap."

"Yeah, well, you haven't seen me eat yet."

Elizabeth bowed her head and clasped her hands. "Dear Lord, bless this food and us to Your loving service. Amen."

"Rub-a-dub-dub. Thanks for the grub. Yeah, God," Jordan contributed. "What's your prayer, Mr. Blake?" She gave him an expectant look.

Blake shifted in his chair. That had been his prayer at the dining room table when he'd still believed there was a God. His mother had been great with prayers, always knowing what to say and how to say it. His tongue twisted inside his mouth, but no sound came out. He stared at the equipment stationed by Jordan's bed and the IV line attached to her arm. Asking for God to heal

Jordan didn't seem to be an appropriate thing to say at dinnertime.

As if understanding his discomfort, Elizabeth put her hand on her daughter's arm and squeezed. "Now, Jordan, Blake doesn't need to say his own prayer. I think ours covered him, as well. Let's eat. I'm starving."

Thankful to be out of that tight situation, Blake grabbed for his dinner and ate it directly out of the carton. "Tell me—what's your favorite subject in school?"

"Well, I like to read and study about what happened in the past." Jordan slurped up a noodle.

"Reading is good. And so is learning history so we don't make the same mistakes." Blake would do well to follow his own advice, he thought as Elizabeth smiled at him. "What about you, Elizabeth?"

"Biology and chemistry, of course."

Blake suddenly had a hard time concentrating on the piece of chicken in his mouth as he watched Elizabeth. Despite his resolve not to get involved, he wondered what it would be like to kiss her.

He swallowed hard and almost choked. The doctor wasn't his type, and after his disastrous marriage to Tessa, he shouldn't even be thinking about the adoptive mother of his child. Or worse yet, the widow of his late father's protégé, who had a better relationship with his dad than he had.

"What was yours, Mr. Blake?"

"Lunch and gym."

Jordan laughed. "Lunch isn't a subject."

"Tell that to my stomach. Watch this." Blake took a piece of chicken and flung it into the air above his head. He heard Elizabeth and Jordan both gasp and it almost upset his concentration. He hadn't done this in years, and the food had gone higher than he'd anticipated—he hoped it didn't come down on the sheets or worse yet, someone's head. Keeping the chicken in his line of sight, he almost upset their makeshift table as he managed to catch the morsel in his mouth, much to his daughter's delight.

Jordan's squeals filled the room and made him smile. Seeing the joy on her face lifted his heart.

"You're right. I guess lunch was a subject for you." Elizabeth lost the battle against laughing, sending a wave of emotion through him that he was afraid to identify. He had a hard time not staring at the beautiful doctor, and wanted to slide his chair closer to her so he could bask in her glow.

"Watch this." Jordan placed a noodle between her lips and slurped. The long pasta whipped around, leaving a trail of sauce along her cheeks and chin.

"Nice job. We'll move on to bigger food groups when you're well."

"You'll still be here, then?" Jordan slurped up another noodle.

"Of course I will."

Elizabeth panicked as Blake turned to her, his expression pleading with her to tell Jordan who he was. Indecision tore at her and she rolled her head from side to side, trying to release the tension.

Suddenly Jordan squealed in delight. "It's The Boston Brothers! Quiet, please."

Saved by the commercial for the upcoming concert.

He shifted his gaze back to Jordan and had to stop himself from grabbing her hand. What would it feel like to weave Jordan's fingers through his? Sure he'd held children's hands before to comfort them, but holding the hand of his daughter, a child who carried his DNA, would be—he wasn't sure how the moment would feel. Awe inspiring? Incredible? Frightening? Humbling?

Jordan gave her mom a pleading look. "Mom? Can I, please?"

Elizabeth squeezed her daughter's hand. "I'm sorry, sweetie. Not this time."

Lightness filled Blake's heart as he remembered his plan. If they couldn't take her to the concert, maybe they could bring the concert to her.

Once they'd collected the trash and stuffed it back into the plastic bag, Elizabeth rose to her feet and pulled off the tablecloth as Blake moved the chair back into the corner. Her hand touched Jordan's forehead again before she leaned down and gave her a kiss and handed her the phone. "Here. Call Taylor and tell her all about your dinner. I'll be back in a bit to tuck you in and say good-night."

Blake couldn't deny that Elizabeth was a good mother. Tessa had made the right decision in picking the doctor to raise his daughter. His own mother had known what he'd needed and was always there for him. Maybe that was all it took to be a good father. He grabbed the chair he'd pulled from the break room in one hand and the garbage in the other, tucking those thoughts in his head. "I'll go put this back."

He communicated with a nudge of his head for Elizabeth to follow him.

They entered the break room. A low-back, tan couch and a recliner huddled around a small television, and a fake ficus tree was stationed in the corner. A fresh pot of coffee sat on the white counter. Elizabeth helped herself to a cup. "Coffee?"

"No, thanks." Blake held up the remains of his soda.

Elizabeth joined him at the table as Blake took a piece of paper from his pocket and unfolded it, smoothing out the creases. Elizabeth stared at his long, lean fingers, and thought about how he'd struggled to come up with a prayer. If only he would find God—then he'd understand his purpose and find the inner peace that apparently eluded him.

"I did some research online today about donating bone marrow and talked to the local reps from the marrow registry. The process is easy. Finding funding for those who can't afford the fee to be typed and added to the registry, and getting the word out, is going to be the challenge."

Hope filled Elizabeth again. With her and Blake working together to find the solution, they would succeed. Even though Blake didn't believe, she knew God had brought them together. "I can ask my friend, Susie, for help. Her sister works for Channel 10. She knows a lot of people and can probably get us lots of coverage."

"That's great, but it won't do us much good if they can't afford the fees involved."

"We'll find the money." Elizabeth set her hand over Blake's and squeezed gently. She thought of her rapidly depleting bank account and closed her eyes. Faith had gotten her this far, and she would continue to lift up her prayers to Him. She opened her eyes and stared at their clasped hands, feeling a surge of compassion, awareness and love? No. It was just her heightened emotions. She took her hand off his. "What else is on the list?"

"Finding a space big enough where we can stay for at least four hours." Blake paused for a second and let out a deep breath. "We can do it at Desert Light Church on Shea a week from Saturday. I met the pastor, Mark Ferguson, here when I went in for my testing and have already spoken to him."

Elizabeth's heart filled with joy. While it wasn't a direct confession, Blake had opened the doors to accepting God. It wouldn't happen overnight, but maybe over time. *Thank You, Lord.* "That's a bigger church. It will work better for us. What else do we need?"

"The church has tables and chairs, but we're going to need some volunteers to help. The National Bone Marrow Donor Program will also send in two people, but most of it will fall on our shoulders."

"Okay. I'm sure between the two of us, we'll find plenty of volunteers."

"We'll also need to pass out flyers and get the media coverage you talked about earlier to publicize the event and broaden our range. It sounds like we could be in for a battle trying to find a match because of Jordan's tissue type."

Elizabeth's newfound hope sputtered like a sparkler on the Fourth of July. She shot up from the table and paced the tiles. After a few moments, she turned to face him, her arms across her chest, desperation in her eyes. "I don't know what to do anymore."

He gathered her to him and held her close. She felt right in his arms, as if she belonged there. The staccato beating of her heart complemented his and she found it hard to remember why she shouldn't get involved with her daughter's father. "Keep praying. We will find someone, Elizabeth."

"I know we will. And maybe it will have something to do with Tessa. I still get this feeling I should be contacting someone from her side, whether it's her adoptive parents or from her biological side."

"I know. I feel it, too. Have you ever met them?"

Elizabeth shook her head. "The only time they ever came to visit, I was away with Tom."

"Probably a good thing. They're—they can be difficult. I found their number but will have to keep looking for her biological family. I'll be there with you every step of the way." Blake pulled out another piece of paper from his pocket and handed it to her along with his cell phone. "Because Jordan has yours."

Elizabeth's mouth went dry and her fingers shook as she picked up Blake's cell phone. She dialed the number before she talked herself out of it. She wouldn't waste any opportunity, no matter how far-fetched, to find a way to help her daughter.

Their daughter.

The phone rang three times before a woman picked up and cleared her throat. "Hello?"

Elizabeth found her voice and managed to keep the tremors at bay. She gave Blake a half smile as he moved in behind her and placed his hands on her shoulders. "May I speak with Catherine Pruitt, please?"

"This is she. How may I help you?"

"Hi, my name is Elizabeth Randall. I was Tessa's roommate for a year at Harvard."

"Tessa's dead," the woman responded flatly.

Elizabeth stared at the bouquet of roses someone had left in the break room, beautiful to look at but full of thorns. She suspected the woman on the other end of the line was a bit like those flowers and was glad Blake was with her. "I know that, Mrs. Pruitt. My condolences. I wish I could have made the services, but I had a family emergency here in Phoenix." Jordan. Inhaling sharply, she gripped the phone harder, her stomach lurching as she tried to figure out the best approach. "I'm calling in regard to her daughter, Jordan."

"Tessa didn't have any children."

Elizabeth put her hand on her stomach to still the fluttering inside. "Yes, she did. I adopted her at birth. I have a birth certificate and adoption papers to prove it."

"Tessa didn't have any children. Take your extortion attempts and go away."

"I don't want any money. She's got leukemia and we're trying to find a marrow donor for her. I thought you should know."

"Tessa didn't have any children. Good day, Ms. Randall. Go find someone else to harass." After a brief moment of silence, she pulled the phone away from her ear and stared at it in disbelief.

"I'm sorry, Elizabeth. They've always been like that."

Disappointment welled inside her at Tessa's mother's response.

* * *

"How's Taylor doing?" Elizabeth tucked her phone away before she sat on Jordan's bed. Her daughter looked a bit more settled after her talk with her best friend. Having Thai food had probably helped, too. She was grateful to Blake for their picnic.

"She's okay. They just adopted a new kitten. She can't wait for me to come over and see it." The more Jordan had something to look forward to, the better she would feel. Her gaze caught Blake's.

"I can't wait either. Did she tell you what it looks like?"

"It's an orange tabby. Can I have a kitten? She says they are so much fun and really cuddly."

"We have a stray that we feed at the station. How about when you're better, I'll bring you by and you can pet him—he's really friendly. Then you can sit in the truck and the ambulance."

"Really? Can I, Mom?"

"I don't see why not. Now it's time to brush your teeth and go to sleep."

"Aw, Mom, that's all I seem to do. Can't I stay up a little longer?"

"Your mother is right. Sleep helps the body heal. Good night, Jordan."

"Good night, Mr. Blake. Thanks for the picnic."

"You're welcome." Slipping from the room, he heard the rustle of sheets as Jordan rose from her bed with the help of Elizabeth.

Mr. Blake. His daughter should be calling him Dad, but he understood Elizabeth's fears. He'd seen the steady decline in his daughter in the past two weeks. But couldn't he be the source of hope for her? Jordan wanted a father—okay, she also wanted a new husband for her mom—but if she knew who he really was, could it tilt the tables in a new direction? All her infections weren't good and he'd learned from research that even if they found a match, if she wasn't well enough, a bone marrow transplant would be out of the question.

A few minutes later, Elizabeth exited the room and leaned against the wall. With her eyes closed, a vulnerable shadow crossed her features. Blake pulled her to him in comfort and held her.

Underneath the scent of disinfectant, he smelled the slightest hint of vanilla as her soft, wavy hair tickled his cheek. He'd vowed never to get involved emotionally with another woman after Tessa had left him. Yet here he stood with the adoptive mother of his child in his arms—and he didn't mind at all.

Elizabeth began to cry softly. The burden she'd faced alone was destroying her from the inside out. If it didn't stop, she'd be nothing but a shell. He tightened his grip and rocked her gently. "We will get through this, Elizabeth."

"I know." Her tight voice belied her words. If Elizabeth gave up...

He tilted her chin up and saw the same look he probably wore reflected in her eyes before his lips descended on hers.

Chapter Eight

Blake ignored rational thought as his mouth found Elizabeth's and she returned his kiss. Her lips made him temporarily forget the demons set on destroying their daughter.

Kissing Elizabeth hadn't even entered his thoughts when he'd suggested dinner, but now his mind went blank and all he could do was relish her touch and the tenderness he felt behind it. He deepened the kiss, trying to rationalize his actions—he was simply offering comfort.

Right. A hug did that just fine—kissing crossed the line.

Pulling her closer, he allowed his fingers to touch the soft fabric of her white shirt. The warmth of her skin began to erase the emptiness of the past few years that had made him take ridiculous chances and take every adrenaline-junkie opportunity that had crossed his path. Her touch grounded him in the here and now. Kissing her was the right thing to do.

Blake heard the squeak of sneakers on the floor heading toward them and reluctantly lifted his head. Jordan's nurse smiled at him before she walked into the room. The coziness dissipated into the sterile atmosphere, laden with the underlying scent of antiseptic and the low hum of equipment in the background. They were in the hallway—what had he been thinking?

"That was Rebecca, wasn't it?" Color infused Elizabeth's cheeks, yet her eyes remained closed.

"Yes." He watched her struggle to compose herself. He'd been inside enough hospitals to know that by morning the entire staff would have heard that the stoic and formidable Dr. Randall was found in a lip-lock with Jordan's father in the hallway on the fourth floor.

Great. He'd just kissed Elizabeth Randall. Jordan's mother. His father's protégé, Thomas Randall's widow. Now he knew he was certifiable. On his day off tomorrow, he needed to find something crazy to do to get his focus off her. Maybe the high-speed racing school had a last-minute opening, or Eric would want to go parachuting with him.

Elizabeth opened her eyes, and backed off. Confusion replaced the warmth and sparkle he'd seen earlier. Straightening her shoulders, she wiped her lips with her fingertips, stepped backward and then stared at him boldly. "Please don't let that happen again."

Sleep eluded Elizabeth that night. By the next morning, exhaustion had become an intimate friend. But not as intimate as the kiss she'd shared with Blake. Why had she responded to him that way? She should have hauled off and slapped him for taking such liberties, yet she'd kissed him right back.

Was she really that attracted to him? They had a connection because of Jordan, but was that it? Or did her reaction have a deeper meaning? Butterflies filled her stomach and heat scorched her cheeks.

Having Blake around wasn't good for her peace of mind, especially when she had to focus on her daughter and her patients.

At the hospital, Elizabeth pulled a chart and glanced at it quickly before she knocked on the partially open door and smiled at the seven-year-old boy and his parents waiting in the room. "Hi. I'm Dr. Randall. You must be Ethan."

The towheaded boy nodded, his blue eyes round, the skin on his face pale with pain. He held an ice pack to his arm, and even at this angle, Elizabeth could tell his arm was broken.

She sat down on the stool and rolled it closer. "Let me guess. You were climbing a tree in your front yard and fell."

Ethan nodded again, tears welling in his eyes. "I was trying to get Fred out of the tree. The neighbor's dog scared him."

Gently removing the ice pack, she touched the boy's arm, felt up and down, and guessed it was a clean break. "That was very noble of you, but next time, instead of doing it yourself, you need to call your parents or the fire department."

An image of Blake sprung to mind and she instantly felt his lips on hers again. He had dominated every conversation, every waking moment and every thought since the kiss. Fortunately she hadn't seen him since then, but that didn't mean she wasn't aware that he'd already stopped by to see Jordan. Jordan's nurse, Rebecca, had made it a point to tell her so.

Focus. She ruffled the boy's hair. "Now, I'm going to send you upstairs to get an X-ray. Have you ever had one before?"

"No."

"It's really quite exciting. What they do is take a picture of the inside of you. That way I can see where your arm is broken. My daughter would break her arm every week if she could get an X-ray." Pain radiated inside Elizabeth at the thought of Jordan. Her daughter had broken her arm falling from her bike. At the time, Elizabeth had been upset by the fact she hadn't prevented that accident. Now that accident seemed like nothing.

"Really? She likes X-rays?"

Forcing her gaze back to the blond boy, Elizabeth chastised herself—focus on your patient.

"Really. Actually, though, I think it's the cast. It all depends on what the X-ray shows, but I think you're going to need one, so you'll be very popular tomorrow morning when you go to school. Here's a piece of trivia your friends won't know. Do you know why cats get stuck in trees?"

Ethan shook his head again.

"It's because their claws curve and point backward. Great for going up, not so great for coming down. So next time Fred decides to take a climb, call your mom or dad, or better yet, keep him in the house where he belongs." Elizabeth smiled and winked at the boy as the intern with the wheelchair arrived outside the room.

"Now, are you ready for your X-ray?" She pulled a sucker out of her lab coat pocket and looked at Ethan's mother. "May I?"

With the mother's permission, Elizabeth handed Ethan the sucker and the ice pack. "Mr. Hensley is going to take you upstairs for your X-ray and then bring you back down, okay?"

"'Kay."

"Think about your favorite color for your cast. Just not too dark or you won't see all the girls' signatures on it." The boy grinned as she lifted him down from the examining table. Her pager chirped. Another patient was arriving.

Elizabeth strode back to the station. "What have we got?"

Lidia, the nurse behind the counter, glanced up from her paperwork. "Inbound toddler. Started choking and lost consciousness at the day care center. Room 5's open."

"Thanks." Meningitis? Overdose? Head injury? Numerous scenarios flitted through her mind but she praised the Lord at least it wasn't a drowning, which was too common in the Phoenix area. The glass doors to the outside slid open and the paramedic and EMT wheeled the stretcher inside. Elizabeth's breath hitched. Blake. She'd recognize his cropped brown hair and the breadth of his shoulders anywhere. He looked so handsome dressed in his full gear and in action that it almost wasn't fair.

Elizabeth met the crew halfway into the interior. Standing only a few feet away from Blake brought back memories of last night and how she'd responded to his kiss. And how if she had the chance, she'd kiss him again. Somehow, he'd managed to get past the wall around her heart and crack open her mind to the possibility of exploring another relationship with a man. That scared the daylights out of her.

"Let's take her to Room 5." Her gaze remained on the redheaded child with the pigtails—her face pale, her thumb in her mouth, lying on a stretcher made for an adult—as they wheeled her into the room. Tucked inside the crook of her arm was a teddy bear dressed like a fireman, intended to soothe the child's anxiety during the ambulance ride, which made her job somewhat easier.

"I thought you were off today," she said.

"Stephano got sick."

A tiny smile pulled at Elizabeth's lips and she fought hard not to glance into Blake's eyes. She touched her patient's forehead. Clammy. "Hi, I'm Dr. Randall."

The girl sucked her thumb even harder.

"Her name's Meredith," Blake answered, moving the child from the stretcher to the hospital bed. Then he held the little girl's hand. She watched him gently rub the back of it with his thumb, the action endearing him to her even more. He would make a great father. Why couldn't he see it? "The day care director followed us and is in the lobby. She can answer any questions."

"Parents?"

"On their way."

"Well, Meredith, you're in good hands here at Kingfisher. We're going to look you over and make sure everything's fine, okay?" Elizabeth continued to stroke the girl's forehead. Some color started creeping back into the toddler's cheeks.

Meredith nodded and opened her eyes, which were glassy. Her body was still lethargic. "History?" she asked Blake.

"Meredith was eating a breadstick. She started gagging, and according to one of the girls in the room, her eyes rolled back in her head and she lost consciousness. The staff managed to dislodge the piece of bread, but Meredith remained unconscious. My guess is a fibril seizure. She was lethargic and feverish when we arrived."

"Thanks." Elizabeth's focus never left the child. "Meredith, first I'm going to check your eyes." She pulled out her small light and shone it in the girl's eyes—dilated. "Now I'm going to feel your pulse." She picked up her wrist—shallow and rapid. "And now your heartbeat." She lifted the princess shirt up and placed her stethoscope on the girl's chest—nothing out of the ordinary. Meredith perked up a bit and tried to grab the stethoscope from Elizabeth's hand.

"Do you want to hear?"

Meredith nodded, so Elizabeth let her listen to her heartbeat.

"Nice observation, Blake—fibril seizure is my guess, too. You'd make a great doctor."

"I only knew because I've run across this scenario before." She lost the battle not to look at him, noticing the light growth of hair along his chin and jawline. Inhaling sharply, she took in the light scent of fresh soap and sunshine. Another funny feeling took hold. His blue eyes stared down at her and it looked like another thought hovered on his lips, yet he bit the words back. She looked away.

"Okay, Meredith. We're going to keep you here a bit. We want to make sure everything's fine." Elizabeth picked up the little girl's hand and patted it gently. "Someone go get the day care director to stay with her. Let me know when her parents arrive."

Elizabeth followed Blake out of the room. As she made some notes on the girl's chart, she saw Corey motion to Blake that he was going to the cafeteria. Would Blake use the opportunity to go see Jordan again?

Elizabeth wished she could run upstairs, too, but she didn't have enough time before Ethan came back from X-ray, and she figured Meredith's parents would be showing up any minute.

Wandering into the break room, she grabbed a cup and filled it with cold water from the dispenser. As she drank, she realized it was time—she had to tell Jordan the truth about her adoption and about Blake's identity. The longer she waited, the harder it got. Watching Blake with Meredith today—and with Jordan since he'd met her—she knew he had what it took to be a dad. He'd be great with Jordan. So what was she worried about?

Restlessness propelled her back into the main area. The man who dominated her thoughts now stood with the empty stretcher by the main entrance, waiting for Corey, his head down, his fingers wrapped around the metal bars along the side. Even from this distance, she could feel his tension.

Her feet made short work of the space between them and she put her hand on his shoulder. "Are you okay?"

"Fine. I just—never mind."

They'd discussed it briefly, but Elizabeth wondered if dropping out of med school bothered him even though he denied wanting to be a doctor. "Look, if it's what I said—"

"It's not that."

"You would make a good doctor. You care about people, Blake."

Blake scraped a hand across his face. "When are you going tell her, Elizabeth? It's been a week. My patience is running low."

"I—I'll—" Elizabeth ran her fingers up and down the tubing of her stethoscope.

"You're afraid," Blake said gently.

Elizabeth avoided looking into his knowing eyes. She *was* afraid but not for the reason she'd mentioned earlier. She wasn't protecting Jordan—she was protecting herself.

"Mom, can I ask you a question?" Jordan asked Saturday afternoon as she pulled the wooden stick out from the Jumbling Tower game and carefully placed it on top crossways. The stack of blocks trembled slightly but didn't fall over.

"Sure. Ask away." Elizabeth tapped her lips, looking for a stick that wouldn't upset the stacked bocks. In the beginning, she used to let Jordan win. Now, it was a challenge not to lose to her too early. She tapped a stick lightly until it gave enough so that she could extricate it.

"Am I adopted?"

Elizabeth's fingers slipped and bumped into the tower. Blocks jumbled over and bounced on the surface of Jordan's bed tray. Some even fell to the floor. She gasped to fill her lungs and calm the frantic beating of her heart.

Had Blake managed to tell his daughter before she did? He'd said his patience was low, but he wouldn't, would he? He'd still been in the hospital when Meredith's parents came and she had to go take care of Ethan's arm. He could have easily run upstairs and seen Jordan.

No. She had to believe he would honor his word. Besides, Jordan would have said something last night.

"What makes you ask that?" Elizabeth started to clean up the mess. She focused on placing the blocks three in a row, not on her daughter's inquisitive face.

"I heard Rebecca talking when she didn't think I was listening. It's not true, is it?" Tears filled her daughter's eyes. "I'm your daughter, right?"

Elizabeth couldn't deny the truth anymore. Her hand had been forced, as she'd known it would be eventually.

Pushing the table out of the way, she moved a few blocks from the blanket and settled down on the bed next to Jordan.

"Yes, you are my daughter, honey. And I'll always be your mom." She inhaled deeply and gave Jordan a fractured smile. Tears stung the back of her eyes. If only she had a way to keep the sting of her words from devastating her daughter. "I just didn't give birth to you like other moms do. I adopted you because I loved you long before you were born. And I still do love you. Nothing's changed."

"Why didn't you tell me?"

Picking up Jordan's hand, Elizabeth squeezed it gently. The tears filling her daughter's eyes wrenched her deeply. Jordan didn't need this kind of stress in her condition, but Elizabeth couldn't avoid the truth anymore. "Your biological mother didn't want you to know."

"Why?"

She dried a tear from Jordan's cheek with her thumb, wishing she could absorb the pain. "I think it's because she was adopted herself and she knew at an early age. It bothered her and she wanted to spare you the hurt."

"So you know who my real mom is?"

Elizabeth continued to cling to Jordan's hand. "It was Auntie Tessa."

"Auntie Tessa?" A fresh batch of tears spilled over her lids. "Auntie Tessa was my mother? But—I don't understand."

"We'd been friends a long time. She loved you. She couldn't keep you, yet she wanted to be a part of your life."

"And now she's dead and I'll never—"

Elizabeth reached out and wrapped her arms around her daughter's shoulders. "Jordan, I'm sorry. I can't go back and make this go away. It's what she wanted. Nothing's changed, though. She loved you. I love you and your dad loved you."

"You mean my adopted dad. Do you know who my

real dad is?" Breaking away, Jordan folded her bony arms in front of her.

Her daughter's words cut deeply. It didn't matter if she had no biological connection to Tom—he had loved her. She was their daughter. But Elizabeth swallowed the lump in her throat and nodded. "It's Mr. Blake."

"Mr. Blake?" More sobs broke from her lips. "And he knew, too?"

Nodding, Elizabeth tried to gather Jordan in her arms again, but her daughter turned away. "He found out only a few weeks ago. That's why he came to find you. He loves you, too."

"So that's why he's been visiting a lot. So when I get better, I'll be going to live with him, won't I?" With a horrified look, Jordan picked up her stuffed bear and sobbed into the soft fur. "But I don't—he—you—you lied to me. All of you. Go away."

This time when Elizabeth wrapped her arms around Jordan again, Jordan didn't pull away. Softly stroking what remained of her daughter's hair, she quietly sang the song she used to sing when Jordan was a colicky baby.

"I'm not going away, darling. Never," she said.

Not as long as she could help it.

Elizabeth's hands shook as she knocked on the station door later that afternoon. If he wasn't here, she prayed that one of his coworkers would give her his address. She'd finally managed to get an exhausted Jordan to take a nap so she couldn't stay away too long. Too bad she hadn't been able to take a snooze herself.

In her room, all she did was pace until the four walls crowded out the remainder of her sanity. She should have called Susie, but instead she drove to see Blake. Somehow she knew he'd understand.

The door opened, revealing Jordan's father. His shirt was wrinkled, as if he'd been sleeping. "Elizabeth? Come in." He held the door open farther and ushered her inside. "What's wrong? Is it Jordan?"

"I'm sorry. I didn't realize you'd be—she's fine, it's—it's—" Fresh tears filled her eyes and choked her voice. She sounded like a crazed woman. Jordan's reaction shouldn't have been a surprise, yet it was—especially her last words.

"We're used to interruptions. Comes with the job. Busy night last night. Today hasn't been much better, I'm afraid." He laced his hand through hers and tugged her toward the kitchen. She liked the feel of his palm against hers—it had been so long since she'd felt a companionship with anyone.

"The E.R. was crazy, as well. I heard ambulances arriving at all hours last night."

"Yeah. I think we were at Kingfisher twice. I'll make some coffee." He settled her into a chair and went to work at the counter, giving Elizabeth a chance to study him again. Broad shoulders and strong arms made to carry the weight of any situation. He'd been instrumental in getting the bone marrow drive set up for next Saturday. And in keeping Jordan company while Elizabeth worked. And in just being there for her, like now. A familiar emotion tugged at her heart.

He placed the cup in front of her along with some

cream and different kinds of sweetener. Then he filled one for himself. He pulled out his chair and sat down next to her. "You told Jordan, didn't you?"

"She overheard Rebecca talking and asked me about it." She rested her forehead on her fisted palm.

He reached out and took her free hand. "I take it the news didn't go well."

"Like an empty box at a birthday party." His gentle touch comforted her and reminded her she was no longer alone. She really wanted to let Blake hold her, but friends didn't act that way.

Somewhere along the way, she'd developed feelings for Blake, but that didn't mean she was ready to have a relationship. And Blake took risks, and his job had the potential to put his life in jeopardy every day. Plus, he'd made baby steps toward believing but hadn't committed himself to the Lord.

Could she try with Blake? Should she?

No quick answer sprang into her brain. All she knew was that with Blake in their lives, nothing would ever be the same again.

"Which part didn't go well? The adoption or me?"

"Neither." Her neck tensed and the pounding in her head increased. Elizabeth began to massage her temples, Jordan's words echoing in her mind. "She accused both of us of lying and told me to go away."

"I'm sure she didn't mean that." Blake stood and moved around behind her. He began to massage her neck and shoulders. At his touch, the pain subsided a fraction. "She's scared. She needs you more than ever now."

"I know that. But what if I made a mistake?"

"Relax, Elizabeth. We have to look ahead and do what's best for her from this day forward. What was Jordan doing when you left?"

"Sleeping." Somehow just being in Blake's company, sharing her pain and fears alleviated some of her tension. So did his massage. Until the realization that she had fallen for him took her breath away.

"So we have some time. I'd rather not talk about it here. Let's go get something to eat and think about something else for a while."

"Aren't you working?"

"I filled in for Matt so he could go watch his son's baseball game. He came back a few hours ago. I was just catching up on sleep before I went to the hospital to see Jordan."

Elizabeth searched Blake's face. "I'm terrified, Blake."

"It'll be okay, Elizabeth. We're going to figure this all out. Trust me."

Chapter Nine

Bright sunlight spilled around them as they stepped outside the fire station. After the chill from the air-conditioning inside the building, the heat felt good. Blake put his sunglasses on and turned to face her. "What do you feel like eating?"

"I'd rather go back to the hospital if you don't mind."

He cupped her elbow and led her to her car before he turned to face her. "I do mind. Look, I know you're hungry and that you're subsisting on cafeteria food. That's not good enough to keep you healthy and one step ahead of Jordan's leukemia. I know of a good burger joint. They have homemade frozen custard, too. We can bring one back for Jordan for dessert."

"That wouldn't be any more healthy than the hospital food." She cracked a smile.

"True, but the atmosphere is much better for the spirit. Now which car should we take?"

"Okay, you win. Let's drop my car off at the hospital."

Twenty minutes later, Blake pulled up in front of a

white building with red-and-white striped awnings. A big 3-D custard cone dominated the front and Tillie's Steakburger blazed in big red letters. Elizabeth's stomach rumbled—Blake's words rang true. Outside of the Thai food, and dinner out with Susie last week, she'd lived on the cafeteria food. She prayed that she could take Jordan home soon and start cooking again.

"I've heard good things about this place. I've passed by here a few times but never stopped in."

"You've missed out. Trust me, you won't be disappointed." Blake held the door open for her, allowing the cool temperatures and mouthwatering aroma from inside to swirl around her.

"Jordan would love this place." A hint of guilt laced her voice as she noticed a small arcade section by the take-out area. She should be with Jordan, not having dinner with Blake.

Blake sensed her disquiet. "When Jordan gets healthy, there will be plenty of time to bring her here."

Elizabeth nodded, liking his use of the word *when,* not *if.* And she had to admit, the atmosphere was much better than the stark walls of the cafeteria even though burgers and fries wasn't the healthiest meal she could eat. She spied the two big machines churning out vanilla and chocolate custard to the left of the cashier.

"Hi. Welcome to Tillie's. May I take your order?" The perky, dark-haired teenager greeted them from behind the front counter.

"Sure." Elizabeth perused the old-fashioned handwritten sign announcing their custom-burger options. After she placed her order, she took in the red-and-white checked tiles that graced the wall behind the counter. Cooks in long white aprons and white paper hats worked behind the grills and cut the fries. It was a pretty, cheerful place—Jordan would love it.

The seating area was just as quaint with its red chairs and white tables. Blake held her chair after he set his soda down on the table. It was the little things that made her miss being in a relationship, she realized—the things she'd taken for granted when her husband was alive.

Sitting next to the wall covered with old pictures filled her with more nostalgia. "This place is really neat. I'm sorry I missed it all these years."

"It's been around since the fifties. Those pictures are authentic." His fingers played with the red-and-white striped straw, drawing it in and out of his drink. "My mom used to bring me here before she died."

"Would it be too forward of me to ask what happened?" She placed her hand on his arm and squeezed gently. His muscles bunched beneath her palm and he didn't pull away but his gaze never left his drink.

"Cancer."

Elizabeth stiffened. His mother and now his daughter. What if Blake got it?

"How old were you?"

"Ten." From the bitter expression on his face, Elizabeth could tell Blake hadn't accepted his mother's death. If only he would put his faith in God and let Him into his life to share his burdens. Then maybe Blake would find acceptance and peace within. Elizabeth's heart ached for the little boy still inside the man sitting opposite her.

A disembodied voice floated over the loudspeaker. "Number ninety-seven, your order is up."

"Food's ready." Blake pulled his arm away, scraped back his chair from the table and stood. Elizabeth followed his movements as he walked to the front. His slow gait spoke volumes. Not only did she want to heal Jordan, but she wanted to help Jordan's father, as well.

Elizabeth bit into her patty melt and let the juicy flavor tickle her taste buds. It had been a long time since she'd had such a tasty burger. "This is good. So tell me, Blake, what other icons have I missed in the Valley?"

"Well, there's Encanto Park over in Phoenix and if you're adventurous, there's always Greasewood Flats. It used to be way out there, but the city has encroached around it."

"Encanto Park? Greasewood Flats? Sounds like I've missed a lot."

"You were busy establishing your career."

"True." Elizabeth thought she heard censure in his voice. She knew it related to his father and not necessarily her. Or did it? Having been on the fast track her entire life, she questioned the things she might have missed besides a steakburger at Tillie's.

She took another bite and savored the flavor. "What's your favorite spot?"

"Lately, it's parasailing out by Lake Pleasant, but when I was a kid, it was riding the carousel on the Enchanted Island at Encanto Park. Another place my mom used to take me. After she died, all the excursions stopped."

"Your dad never took you anywhere?"

Blake shook his head and chewed slowly. "Everything stopped. He never recovered from my mom's death, either. The joy went out of both our lives. I sometimes wonder what would have happened if she hadn't died."

Silence prevailed as Elizabeth chewed on her French fry. The delight in her food dissipated quicker than a box of donuts in the staff lounge. More pain etched its way into her heart for both the man and the boy he used to be. She couldn't relate, having lost her dad and then her mom in her twenties.

"Please don't beat yourself up about the would haves and could haves. Sometimes I don't understand His will or the plans He has for each one of us, but I do know that He loves us and wants what's best for us."

Blake shifted on his chair, his gaze on her, his expression between confusion and contempt. "I'm not sure I believe that. So what did you do for fun growing up in Henderson?"

Elizabeth let him change the subject. "The usual. I rode my bike. Went swimming. Shopping." This time Elizabeth toyed with her straw.

"Did you like it there?"

"It was okay. I didn't really have any friends except Tom, who was a family friend. My parents were older and immigrants from Poland. I didn't even speak English until I went to school. I was different and smart. Being the only fifteen-year-old in the graduating class put a damper on friendships and invitations to the class parties."

"Sounds like you need to go out and have some fun to make up for it."

"I can't argue there."

"So the talk about you is true. You're a genius."

"I scare most of my coworkers." A mixture of hurt and amusement flickered in her eyes.

Blake picked up her hand and entwined his fingers through hers. He rubbed her hand against his cheek, his new growth rough against her tender skin. "You don't scare me."

"Well, maybe you should reconsider." His gaze too intense, she took her hand from his, crumpled up her wrapper and placed it on the red tray.

He set his soda cup on the tray and just smiled at her. "Let's go get that custard for Jordan."

As they approached the front of the restaurant, Elizabeth stared at the old-fashioned pinball machine, her fingers touching the cool glass on top.

"I would never have thought this was your thing," Blake spoke over her shoulder.

She could never understand the fascination with arcade games. "It's not but Jordan loves them. It must be all the lights and sounds."

"I used to be a master as a kid." Blake pulled some coins from his pocket. "Excuse me, ma'am." He bowed slightly, gave her a smile and moved into position. His first attempt failed miserably because he couldn't get the flappers to coordinate. His second attempt didn't fare any better.

"A master, huh?"

"It's not as easy as I remember it, Elizabeth. You give it a try." Stepping away from the controls, he guided her into place.

"Okay, but I won't have any better luck than you."

"You can't be any worse." He stood behind her and placed his hands over hers. "When you see the ball coming close, push the buttons and the flappers should bounce it away."

Elizabeth should have been used to his nearness by now, but as she inhaled his clean scent she kept pushing the buttons at the wrong time. His touch didn't help either. Her earlier sensation of wanting to be in his arms returned. What would it feel like to love Blake? To be *in* love with him.

The silver ball came close and Elizabeth pushed the buttons. They moved, shooting up against the bumpers, causing more bells to ring.

"Good job." His ragged whisper filled her ear. It was all she could do not to lean back a fraction, turn her head and graze his lips with hers. Blake made her want love again—for herself, not just for Jordan.

The ball rolled past the flappers and dropped out of sight.

Blake pulled out two more quarters. "Last try? Then we'll go back to the hospital?"

Her gaze locked on the gentle and caring expression in his eyes. Time refused to move forward until she blinked to break the connection and stepped away. "Your turn again."

Blake didn't argue. Shaking his head slightly, he

stepped back up to the controls and scratched his cheek. "Now that I'm warmed up, it should be easier this time."

With the concentration of a skilled surgeon, Blake took control of the game. The points racked up on the screen as more lights lit and bells sounded. She was beginning to see the fascination. "You are really good at this."

Elizabeth cheered him on as he kept pushing the silver ball back into play. More lights flashed and bells sounded and the ball seemed to spin faster with each passing second. She gravitated toward him, wanting to be nearer him and his energy.

"So how long does this go on?"

"Until I lose." He pushed the flappers again, racked up more points and gave her a grin. "Now, if you don't mind, my cheerleading section is a little distracting."

Elizabeth laughed again and moved closer still, glad that Blake wasn't the only distraction around. "You don't give up, do you?"

"No, I don't."

Their gazes froze on each other for a fraction and she knew it had more to do with Jordan than anything. The ball shot back, rolling through the flapper before Blake could respond. He tapped the glass with his fist. He'd just lost, and somehow Elizabeth sensed his frustration had nothing to do with the game. "Come on, let's get that custard and go see Jordan."

As they waited in line, Blake grabbed a white paper napkin and deftly folded it into a flower. He gave her a mock bow. "One of the few things I learned in med school. A rose for a rose." He gave her another grin.

"And the best part is, when you're tired of it, you can use it to wipe your face."

"Thank you, sir." Elizabeth laughed and curtsied before she took the delicate rose.

She couldn't remember the last time she'd had so much fun. And she had Blake to thank for it.

For the first time in a long time, Elizabeth felt lucky.

"Hi, sweetie." Elizabeth ushered Blake into the room. "I've brought someone with me and he's got a treat for you."

"Some frozen custard. Your mom tells me chocolate is your favorite, but I think you'll like this, too. It's my personal favorite." Blake handed her the cup filled with chocolate custard topped with hot fudge, butterscotch, pecans, whipped cream and two maraschino cherries.

His gaze shifted to Elizabeth, and Blake saw her close her eyes, her lips moving as if she were praying for strength. Maybe he should follow her lead—he certainly could use a little help right now.

Jordan stared at him with her big blue eyes, but refused to reach for her dessert. "Thanks. Please put it on the tray—thank you."

"You're welcome." Blake shifted, unsure of his next move. Somehow he hadn't factored in that his daughter might not want *him* to be her father. Wrong. She'd been requesting another one, but in a stepdad capacity. In her mind, Tom had been her father.

For years, Thomas Randall had been Jordan's father, raising her as his own. He'd probably stayed up at night with her. Watched her sit up, utter her first word, take her first step.

Anger and jealousy warred inside Blake. He should have been the one who experienced all that. But in his immaturity, he hadn't been there for Tessa and she'd done the only thing she knew to do.

He stepped up and squeezed his daughter's hand. How small and fragile it felt. Suddenly he felt like a knight in shining armor, weapon in hand, ready to slay the dragon that had robbed his daughter of a normal childhood. They would win. They would find a match for her.

"Look, Jordan, I know you're upset, and both your mom and I are sorry we didn't tell you the truth. It's— Sometimes parents make mistakes, too. Now I'm going to be here for you going forward and working with your mom to get you well. Continue to call me Mr. Blake if you want. I only want you to be okay with whatever decision you make."

Closing his eyes briefly, he tried to infuse some energy and strength into Jordan.

Maybe the pastor at Desert Light had been right. Blake was being given a second chance. He couldn't change the past, but he could change the future. He glanced toward the ceiling, noting only the flecked tiles above. He hadn't really expected to see anything, but inside he felt a shift. An opening. A desire to learn more.

Maybe tomorrow he'd explore the fellowship Mark Ferguson had offered.

As long as Elizabeth went with him.

* * *

Once they'd tucked Jordan in, Blake walked Elizabeth to her temporary quarters on the second floor. He didn't need to go inside to know that the tiny room hosted a twin bed, a dresser and a television. There'd also be a small refrigerator underneath a three-foot counter that had a toaster oven on top of a microwave. Dishes were done in the sink next to the counter and on top of the only cabinet in the place.

His father had had this room when Blake's mother lay dying in the hospital. Even then, William Crawford had left his son in the care of a live-in housekeeper. His father had wanted to spare him the pain of watching her suffer, except it left Blake feeling even more abandoned and rejected than before.

"Good night, Blake. Thanks for everything." Elizabeth leaned over and kissed him, startling Blake from his thoughts. Behind her fatigue, he saw something flare in her eyes as her hand lingered on his arm.

He wasn't ready for the night to end yet. "Do you want to go get a cup of coffee or soda? My treat."

"No, thanks. I'm beat." She eyed him quizzically. "But I get the feeling you want to talk about something. What is it?" She leaned against the door, her lips curving into the smile he'd begun to know so well.

Blake scraped a hand over his head and swallowed his anxiety, knowing he'd made the right decision. Peace started to settle in the empty place in his heart. "I've done some soul searching and I want to know more. I was wondering if you would go to church with me tomorrow."

Surprise lit her face and tears filled her eyes. "Of course I will." She flung her arms around his neck and sealed her promise with another kiss.

And if that wasn't a sign that he was on the right path, he didn't know what was.

"Nervous?" Elizabeth glanced over at him in the Desert Light parking lot.

"A little." Blake's knuckles were white as he gripped the steering wheel. He'd been here twice already, but neither of those times had he stepped foot into the sanctuary. He didn't know what to expect except a lot of people. More cars pulled into the few spots left open near his vehicle. If worse came to worst, he could bail early and no one would notice, he kept telling himself.

"I'm a little bit anxious myself. I'm used to a much smaller church."

"Thanks for coming with me. It means a lot, especially after that conversation a few weeks ago. I'm sorry I said all that—all doctors don't think they're God, just one in particular that I remember." Blake put his hand on the door and pulled the handle.

If he didn't get out now, he'd chicken out. And how would he explain that to Jordan when he saw her? She'd wanted to come with them, but Elizabeth decided she'd had enough excitement for the weekend and should stay in bed. Blake had agreed, not liking the glassiness in his daughter's eyes.

"Don't worry about it."

She squeezed his hand. "I've needed to get back to church, as well. I haven't come since before Jordan's diagnosis. Obviously this isn't the one I normally go to, but it doesn't matter. Where two or more people gather in His name, He is there."

And He was.

Blake felt it almost immediately when he entered the narthex. A sense that he'd come home surrounded him, welcomed him into the fold of people streaming toward the auditorium worship area. Everywhere he looked, another face smiled back at him. It was true—even in denial, God still loved him and forgave him.

Maybe it was time for Blake to do the same.

All those years of pent-up anger at his father began to dissipate. Blake would do anything to keep Jordan from pain, even lay down his life. Under the circumstances, William had done the best he could. He got that now.

He glanced at Elizabeth. "Ready?"

"Ready." Hand in hand, they walked into the sanctuary and found seats near the back. Having Elizabeth with him helped. So did the idea that God was watching out for him and inviting him back to worship. So far, so good. Despite the size of the room, Blake felt an immediate sense of relief as he sat on a chair.

No pews here, and none of the religious icons he usually associated with church. Only a simple, large cross hung from the back ceiling, on a delicate chain. No Bibles or hymn books, only two large screens in the middle of the stage surrounded by potted plants.

In the corner, a woman played the electric piano as the words to the songs flashed on the screens. Churches had changed since his youth, but the messages had not.

He glanced at the program he'd received as Pastor Mark walked onto the stage.

Isaiah was the topic for this morning's service.

Blake's interpretation of being blind was more than just not being able to see. It was like he'd been blindfolded for the last two decades and the blindfold had finally been removed. Like himself, millions of people forged ahead on their daily lives without guidance. But today, his darkness turned to light and in that instant, Blake started to believe again.

For the first time in years, he prayed, finally knowing what to say.

God would not forsake them.

Chapter Ten

Wednesday afternoon had finally arrived. Everything had to be just right. Excitement filled Blake as he stepped into the play area at the end of the hall that took up the entire north side of the building. Good. The band's crew had arrived right on schedule.

If he felt like a kid in the proverbial candy store, what would Jordan and the others feel?

Rebecca joined him on the dark green carpeting that he assumed was supposed to resemble grass, complementing the park scene painted on the walls. "Thanks for arranging this, Mr. Crawford. It'll sure be the highlight of the year, if not the decade. How did you manage it?"

"I know someone at the Dare to Dream Foundation." Blake's gaze wandered around the room and took in the oversized bookshelves that dominated the far wall. A big, comfortable chair sat nearby. Another area was filled with games, and three computers sat on desks not too far away.

Foldable chairs had been placed in a semi-circle in

front of the area where The Boston Brothers' roadies set up their equipment. Blake couldn't believe he'd managed to pull this off. He beamed. This would make Jordan so happy. Not just Jordan, every other child on the fourth floor.

"What's everyone's story here?" he asked Rebecca.

"Some are waiting for transplants." Rebecca nodded her head toward a young Native American boy lounging on the floor with a book in his hand. "That little girl in the blue bandana over there at the first computer has leukemia, like Jordan. We also have a few recovering from serious accidents." A nurse wheeled in a boy with both arms and his chest wrapped in bandages. "Colin's recovering from third-degree burns."

The phone rang at the small desk stationed at the back of the room. "I've got to get that. Thanks again, Mr. Crawford. You're going to make all the kids happy today."

"My pleasure."

Blake whistled as he strolled down the hall to Jordan's room barely containing his smile.

"I've got an early birthday present for you," he said as he helped his daughter from her hospital bed. She'd grown even more fragile in the past few days—the bones in her back were more prominent. His grip tightened around her shoulders and he held her a little closer before he set her in the wheelchair next to her bed.

"Okay, but my birthday's not 'til May 8."

Blake's hands stilled on the arm rests. May 8 was still a few weeks away. What if she didn't make it? His grip tightened. The bone marrow drive was in a few days. They would find somebody.

"This was the only time I could plan this."

"Does my mom know?" Jordan still didn't treat him as if he was her dad. It hurt, though he knew it would probably take some time for her to get used to him. He just had to be patient.

"Not yet, but she will shortly." He tucked the well-worn crocheted blanket around her skinny legs. "Did your mom make your blanket?"

Jordan laughed. "No way, silly. My mom can't sew or knit or do anything but fix kids. Except me, of course."

Blake reached out and touched Jordan's shoulder. This was the second time she'd mentioned her mother's job. How would Elizabeth feel knowing Jordan confided this in her father?

"She would fix you if she could, but leukemia is Dr. Jim's specialty, not your mom's. But your mom and I are both trying. We will find a match, Jordan."

"Thanks." A smile lit her lips, but not her eyes.

"So who made this for you?" Blake touched the blanket.

"My *babcia*."

"*Babcia?*"

"Grandmother. My mom is Polish. *Babcia* lived with us after my dad—I mean, Tom—um, my adoptive father—died."

He couldn't imagine what it would have been like to have a young child and be a new widow at the same time. He marveled at how Elizabeth had managed to keep it together.

"It's okay, Jordan. Tom was your dad. And I'm your dad, too. Just in a different way. It's nice that your mom had some help." Pain radiated from his heart. He should have been there for Jordan from the beginning. He'd make certain he was there for her now.

God willing. Blake closed his eyes and a short prayer his mother had taught him came to him. *Angel of God, my Guardian dear, To whom God's love commits me here; Ever this day, be at my side, To light and guard, To rule and guide.* He would teach it to Jordan some-day, when they had more time.

He wheeled her out of her room and into the hallway.

"Where are we going?"

"To the play area."

"My birthday present is in the lounge? Is it that big?"

He hoped that Elizabeth had gotten his text mes-sage and could meet them. She had no idea The Boston Brothers were playing here this afternoon. He worried about her reaction. He probably should have mentioned it, but that would have taken away the surprise for her, as well. He wanted her to share the joy with Jordan and had purposely arranged for the concert to start around the same time her shift ended.

"Yep, your present is pretty big. I hope you like it." He wheeled her inside, where all the other children on the floor had already been assembled into a semi-circle around the makeshift stage. Drums with The Boston Brothers logo on them, a keyboard and two guitars had been set up along with a small sound mixer.

A squeal erupted from his daughter's lips. She clapped her hands in glee and turned around to face him, pure joy radiating from her face. "The Boston Brothers? You brought me The Boston Brothers?"

"Because you couldn't go see them, I brought them to you. Happy Birthday." He leaned down and kissed his daughter's cheek. The action seemed foreign and yet not so foreign after all. Lightness filled him as he pushed Jordan into the front row and stepped off to the side.

"Oh, Blake." Elizabeth's presence lightened his mood even more as she tucked her arm through his like it was the most natural thing in the world. He loved it.

"You made it."

"How did you manage this?"

"I helped my second cousin build a patio on his house a few years back. His fiancée, Sloane, works for the Dare to Dream Foundation. I told them about Jordan and the other kids here and she talked to their promoter. Luckily the boys were able to come to Phoenix before their concert tomorrow night." He gently patted her hand and turned to look at her. Unchecked tears streamed down her face and spilled off her cheeks.

Elizabeth grinned at him through her tears. "What you've done is—is so wonderful. Look how happy she is."

Even from this angle he could see a smile dominating his daughter's face. She sat forward in her chair and clapped her hands as the three blond boys stepped up to their instruments and joined the drummer and keyboardist already on stage. The kids clapped and cheered wildly. It made him proud to know he'd managed to pull this off for Jordan and all the others in the room.

"Good afternoon, everyone," Shane, the lead singer,

spoke into his microphone. "Thanks for letting us come and perform for you today. We're honored to sing for you because you all rock." He held up a fist. "Ready, boys?"

The other two nodded and the music started, breaking into the expectant pause in the room. Soon, Shane's voice started soft and low, singing of teen love and angst. The crowd behind them increased as more staff became aware of the boys' presence. Soon the room was filled.

He pulled Elizabeth into the corner so they could lean against the wall but still see the makeshift stage.

"They are pretty good, aren't they?" Elizabeth wrapped her arm around his waist and leaned her head against his.

"Yep." Blake held on to her a little tighter as if to keep the moment from slipping from his grasp.

"This is incredible. Thank you."

Neither one of them spoke the rest of the concert. Blake held Elizabeth as she swayed in his arms. He decided that if the moment never ended, he'd be okay with that.

"I understand we have a birthday in the crowd?" Tyler's gaze traveled around the group of kids. The girls in the audience screamed for the fifteen-year-old guitarist.

Jordan waved her hand. "Me!"

"Then what are you waiting for? Come on up!" The singer pulled his guitar from around his neck and stepped into the audience to push Jordan's wheelchair between Justin and Shane. The three boys sang a unique rendition of "Happy Birthday" to her, which made all the adults in the room cry—especially Elizabeth.

Blake liked this emotional side of her. To his knowledge, his father hadn't even cried when Blake's mother died. If William Crawford had grieved, it had been done in private.

Blake rubbed his cheek against Elizabeth's soft hair and breathed in deeply. Images like snapshots in a photo album flipped through his mind. How his father came home grim-faced after work and locked himself in his room. How his faraway look became a constant companion. How sadness consumed him as he looked at his son as if he blamed him for his mother's death.

Or maybe, he realized, it was a look of despair because William Crawford blamed himself for his perceived shortcomings. He could control most of the outcomes in surgery, but he couldn't keep his wife alive.

Another piece of understanding wedged its way past the hurt in Blake's heart and he felt the beginnings of forgiveness.

Finished with their song, each of the brothers gave Jordan a kiss on her cheek. If Blake thought his daughter had been happy before, he'd been wrong. She beamed now, which humbled and moved him and brought moisture to his eyes. Brought to his knees by a boy band and a girl—his daughter.

Tyler, Justin and Shane stayed and talked with all the children on the floor after the show. Even staff sneaked up to get autographs and photos. Elizabeth grabbed her camera to take a picture of Jordan and the boys together for a keepsake in her scrapbook.

After the boys had left the room, Jordan wheeled her way back to him. His heart rejoiced at her happiness. She stood up, threw her arms around his neck and kissed him. "Thanks, Dad."

Dad. He loved hearing that unfamiliar word coming from his daughter's lips. And Blake hadn't thought the day could get any better. Pride filled him as he hugged her back.

"Dr. Randall?" Elizabeth glanced up from the paperwork and eyed the older couple staring tentatively at her.

"Yes?" She signed her name and handed the clipboard back to Lidia, hoping this wouldn't take too long. Her shift was over and she wanted to get back upstairs to see Jordan and celebrate her "early" birthday with a pizza. Schooling her voice so as not to show her frustration, Elizabeth asked, "How may I help you?"

The nicely dressed, gray-haired man glanced at his wife before he held out his hand. "I'm Gerald Pruitt and this is my wife, Catherine."

Elizabeth forced her mouth to remain closed as she shook Gerald's hand. These were Tessa's adoptive parents and Jordan's grandparents? She eyed the impeccably dressed woman with the salon-styled hair and pearls. A delicate air surrounded her, a hesitant look in her watery blue eyes. "Pleased to meet you," she finally said.

"Do you have a few moments?" Gerald tucked his arm through his wife's and gently patted her hand. Even after all these years, Elizabeth could still see the love between the two. Someday she hoped to find that for herself again.

Had she already?

"Of course." No matter how she felt about her earlier conversation with Catherine Pruitt, Elizabeth wouldn't turn her back on them. The fact that they'd come here and sought her out meant something had changed. "Would you like to talk here or the cafeteria?"

"My wife and I could use something to drink. With all the road construction, it took us longer to drive here from Las Vegas than we thought."

"Right this way, then."

Five minutes later with drinks in hand, Elizabeth ushered them to a table. No one spoke for a few moments, and Elizabeth had time to collect her thoughts as she blew across the surface of her coffee. Hope blazed underneath her hesitation—they still hadn't mentioned the reason for their visit.

Elizabeth discreetly texted Blake and gave him the news before she wrapped her hands around her foam cup and let its warmth permeate her hands.

"Thank you for not turning us away." Gerald finally spoke. A sheen of moisture gathered on his upper lip despite the air-conditioning inside the big room. Beside him, Catherine nodded.

"You're Jordan's grandparents. I'd never do that."

"We certainly haven't acted appropriately," Catherine whispered. Even her tears were dainty.

"Death has a way of changing people. We had no idea Tessa had a child. Until we found Tessa's photos and Jordan's letters to her." Gerald handed his wife his handkerchief. "Your phone call took us by surprise. We weren't prepared for it."

"I'm sorry for that."

"You had no choice. We understand that now." Gerald reached over and grabbed his wife's hand. "Tessa had been estranged from us for years. We had a fight when she dropped out of med school, and words were spoken in anger. She wanted to live her life on her terms, not under others' expectations for her. About a year later she came back to pick up the rest of her stuff and then disappeared. She only came back into our lives right before she died. It was as if she knew…" Gerald's skin turned ashen.

"But she never spoke of a child. We would never have turned her away. She looked so different. So distraught both times, but I had no idea how to connect with her." Catherine spoke softly. "I was a terrible mother."

"I'm sure you weren't." Elizabeth chose her words carefully. "But by the time Tessa came back to get her things I'd already adopted Jordan. Did you know Tessa was married?"

"She was? And didn't tell us?"

"Yes. I don't know all the details, but she didn't tell him that she was pregnant either. I want you to know that Tessa's ex-husband, Jordan's father, is here and a part of her life now."

Pulling her hands from her husband's, Catherine reached for Elizabeth's. "May we please see our granddaughter?"

"Of course. But there are a few things—"

"You mentioned she has leukemia. How sick is she?" Catherine's grip tightened on Elizabeth's arm.

"She needs a bone marrow transplant."

"Have you found a match yet?" Despite his reserve, Elizabeth heard the desperation in his tone. She knew the feeling well.

"No, we're still looking."

"We're too old to get tested. But there must be something we can do, Elizabeth."

"There is." Elizabeth dug her short nails into her palms. She'd tossed and turned trying to figure out another key factor for the drive on Saturday. Her gaze swept across the older couple again and she knew God had a reason as to why the Pruitts had shown up when they did. Still, she didn't know Tessa's parents well, and hesitated to speak her request.

"What is it? We'll do anything."

Elizabeth dragged in a deep breath. "There's a cost involved to put the people who get tested on the registry. Some can't afford the fees."

"Then we'll pick up the cost. That's the least we can do," Catherine said.

Relief filled her as another piece fell into place. "Thank you. I can't tell you how much that means to me." She glanced at the princess watch Jordan had bought for her last year. "Are you ready to meet Jordan?"

Elizabeth entered the room first, overwhelmed by everything that had happened today. First the concert and now Jordan's grandparents. How would her daughter deal with all the changes?

Better than expected. With her illness and so many new things thrown at her, Jordan had learned to go with the flow.

"Jordan, we have another early birthday present for you," Elizabeth said.

Jordan welcomed her grandparents with elation. "This is so awesome. What should I call you?" Jordan kissed her grandmother on the cheek.

"How about Nana?" Catherine's tears mingled with Jordan's. "And you can call your grandfather Gramps."

"Nana and Gramps. Will you be visiting for a while?"

Tessa's parents looked at Elizabeth, numerous questions in their eyes. "We'll be here for as long as you need us."

Blake hesitated slightly before he entered the room with two boxes of pizza. He'd only heard about Tessa's parents from Tessa, and yet the people standing next to his daughter's bed were a far cry from how she had described them. As he set the pizza down on the tray table, he eyed the elderly couple with reservation, not prepared for the humbleness of their expression.

"Daddy." Jordan held out her arms. He stepped past them and gave his daughter a hug and kiss. "Meet my grandparents."

Blake tweaked her nose before he stood up straight. "Hello, Mr. and Mrs. Pruitt."

"Hello, Blake." Gerald extended his hand. "It's good to finally meet you. Now we can thank you personally."

Blake rubbed his hand across his face, unsure where this conversation was going to lead. "Thank me for what?"

"For giving us a grandchild."

* * *

"Are you sure you want to do this?" Blake held the electric razor in his hand the next morning as he sat in the chair by the bed. He couldn't believe Jordan had asked him to do the honors yesterday. Fear pricked at him. What if he hurt her? What if something went wrong?

He was an EMT. Yet the thought of touching his own daughter—helping to heal her in a different way—made him feel powerless. At times like this, his mother would have turned to the Lord. Elizabeth, too. Still new to his faith, he chose the prayer his mother had taught him.

"Of course I'm sure." Jordan's big brown eyes stared back at him from her hospital bed, her skin still pale from her last round of chemo. While he'd learned that nausea wasn't as bad as it used to be with the procedure, fatigue and bruising were still common as well as infection. His gaze skittered across the IV line in her arm, a dark purple mark blossoming from the site.

Helplessness ravaged him and he needed to find control somewhere. He could only imagine how Elizabeth felt. A pediatric doctor who couldn't help her own child. The irony pierced his soul.

His daughter's fingers bunched the pink-and-purple butterfly comforter, hesitation lingering in her expression. "I can't look any worse than I already do."

"You look beautiful."

"You're just saying that because I'm your daughter."

"No, I'm saying it because it's true." And he meant it. Dark hair, brown eyes and pale moon-kissed skin that reminded him so much of Tessa. He could see a bit of himself in her dimples and the way she angled her head when she spoke. Despite her illness, his daughter always had a ready smile. Jordan was as beautiful on the inside as she was on the outside. "You remind me a lot of your other mom."

"What was she like when you knew her?"

Blake put down the electric razor and picked up his daughter's hand, trying to put some warmth back into her. "Like I said, she was beautiful, like you. Tessa lit up the room with her warm, generous smile. She was smart and funny, and always made me laugh." With his other hand, Blake squeezed the bridge of his nose. The image of Tessa in the justice of the peace's office wearing her simple white sundress and a store-bought bouquet of flowers on their wedding day filled his memory. He'd been so young and naive, not understanding that life was about to throw a few curveballs his way. "I didn't deserve her."

"Why did you get married at all?"

What a question from a kid. "Because I loved her. Or thought I did. I just didn't understand what it took to be a good husband."

"You'll get it right next time, then." She patted his hand and smiled up at him. "Now, let's get this over with. My favorite show is about to start."

Next time.

There wouldn't be one. Marriage took a lot more than just love. All he had to do was look at his coworkers. It took commitment and compromise, the ability to communicate and listen, and to share thoughts and feelings. Respect. Things he didn't have or know how to do.

Blake turned on the electric razor, the buzzing noise filling the room. "Ready when you are."

A few minutes later, what was left of Jordan's hair lay the floor. His hand trembled slightly as he stared at his daughter's bald head. The only adornment on her head now was a pair of tiny emerald studs in her ears and yet her smile never wavered. Blake wished he had her courage. "Okay. My turn."

"Daddy, you don't have to shave your head. Why, you hardly have any hair at all, it's so short."

"Then I won't miss it, will I?" He knelt by her bed so she could have better access. The action reminded him of his enlistment, the only other time he'd sported a buzz job. While this one was a bit more extreme, it was for another great cause. He couldn't think of a better way to support Jordan. His short brown hair mingled with his daughter's long, dark strands on the floor.

It still destroyed him that he couldn't help her physically. Yet deep inside he knew that Jordan's emotional well-being was just as important—his discussion with the nurse earlier confirmed it. They all needed to keep a positive outlook and remain strong.

Elizabeth's gasp met his ears as Jordan shaved the last section of hair from his head. She stopped abruptly inside the threshold, her face paling in the fluorescent light. Her fingers twisted the stethoscope around her neck as she stared at them. Blake watched her struggle to compose herself before she spoke. "Me next?"

"Mom, your hair's too short as it is. Besides, what will you tell your patients? You're supposed to help them not frighten them." Jordan turned off the electric razor. Blake could tell even without looking that his daughter had placed her hands on her hips and pursed her lips.

Leave it to Jordan to tell it as it was. Blake watched the interchange between them with interest, realizing he probably should have told Elizabeth his plans despite the fact Jordan wanted to keep it a secret.

"I could tell them the truth."

"Or you could just grow your hair out. I think it should be longer. This is between my dad and me."

The color left Elizabeth's face and a stricken expression chased away her tentative smile. Stiffly she walked into the room, kissed Jordan's forehead and retreated. "I'm going back to work now. I just ran upstairs to say hi. I'll see you after I get off."

"Elizabeth, wait." Blake shot up from his chair. "I'll be right back, Jordan."

He caught the doctor at the elevator and put his hand on her arm. "I'm sorry, Elizabeth."

"Sorry for what?" Despite her attempts, she couldn't keep the disappointment and pain from her voice.

"I would have asked your permission before I shaved her head, but she asked me not to."

"You're her father. Why should you ask?"

In those few simple words, Blake understood her fears. "I'm not here to take her away from you. We're in this together." He stared into her eyes. "You're her mother. I'm just the new guy on the block right now. She needs you more than ever now."

Moments ticked by as she internalized his words. "How do you know the right thing to say?"

"I spent years saying the wrong thing." He leaned down and gave her a light peck on her lips. "I've still got a long way to go."

The elevator doors opened and another smile graced her lips. "You've come a lot further than you realize."

Chapter Eleven

Saturday dawned bright and sunny, which gave Elizabeth even more hope. God smiled down on her and Blake, and she knew they would get a lead on the person compatible enough to save Jordan at the bone marrow drive today. And in the process, the people added to the registry today could potentially help someone else, like the other girl on the fourth floor who also had leukemia.

The Desert Light Church parking lot teemed with action as Elizabeth pulled her car under a mesquite tree. Cars pulled into the spaces near her and more volunteers along with two coordinators from the bone-marrow organization streamed from their vehicles. She waved at Susie from across the way.

Lightness filled her steps as she entered the building that flanked the main church. It took her eyes a few moments to adjust to the interior and see the sign with the arrow directing her to the right. Three folding tables had been set up for the volunteers to take all the information from the people willing to be tested.

More tables to her right had been set up for the actual testing to take place.

At the far corner, she saw Blake stacking a few boxes of donuts next to a carafe of coffee and some jugs of orange juice. She made her way toward him, acknowledging a few people along the way. Today he was all-powerful and commanding, but just a few days before he had cradled his daughter in his arms with great tenderness. Blake Crawford had many different sides and she was beginning to appreciate all of them.

"Hi. Thanks for organizing all this."

"No problem," he said, giving her a heart-stopping smile. "We need to make sure all our volunteers and donors are taken care of today. The guys from the station are bringing some deli sandwiches at eleven-thirty."

Just before eight o'clock, they were ready. Elizabeth smiled, glancing around the room at the tables filled with volunteers. Her eyebrows raised at the two people sitting together at one of the tables where the potential donors would be swabbed. "Interesting."

"What?" Blake asked beside her.

"Susie and Eric. I had no idea they even knew each other."

"I saw them talking at Dr. Stevens's retirement party, too." He acknowledged the couple with a smile and a wave before he introduced her to the man now standing next to them inside. "You remember Mark Ferguson?"

Elizabeth shook the older man's proffered hand, liking him immediately. Dressed in a Jesus Saves T-shirt and shorts, Mark's firm grip and ready smile offered her measured comfort. "Of course. It's nice to see you again. Thanks for letting us hold the drive here. I think we're going to need the extra space."

"You're welcome. Shall we pray before we open the doors?"

"That would be wonderful." Elizabeth bowed her head and reached for Mark's hand. Joy filled her when Blake grabbed her other one and held on tightly. She squeezed it gently, trying to give him strength.

"Dear Lord, from whom all good gifts flow, we want to thank You today for being here with us and helping Elizabeth and Blake find a compatible donor for Jordan. Guide us and strengthen us as You did Your Son, Jesus Christ. Your will be done. Amen."

"Amen." Elizabeth and Blake spoke together, his voice filled with awe and a bit of surprise, as if waiting for something to happen. Blake had moved in the right direction and Elizabeth was happy for him. She smiled and squeezed his hand again before she let go. "Okay, let's get started."

By the time Blake brought her a sandwich at one, Elizabeth's mouth ached from smiling. She wasn't complaining, though. Far from it. The more people who showed up, the better.

"You looked like you need this. I hope ham and Swiss is okay. We're out of almost everything else."

"I'm so hungry I could eat shoe leather. Can you believe the number of people today?" Elizabeth bit into her sandwich while looking at Blake. Despite all the chaos, he looked calmer than she'd ever seen him.

Blake rubbed his hands across his face before his blue gaze met hers. "Looks like our prayer worked.

It's better than we expected. We're sure to find at least one match."

Ham and cheese never tasted so good. More emotion welled inside Elizabeth. For someone not used to showing her emotions, she felt like a runny faucet these days, and it all had to do with the man sitting on the table. She took in his unshaven face and the laugh lines crinkling around his eyes and mouth. Warmth filled her and another emotion she didn't want to identify.

If she looked too deeply, she'd discover that she cared for Jordan's father a lot more than she should. He made her want the things she'd had with Tom. The closeness, the conversations, the help with Jordan.

A lump formed in her throat, making it hard to swallow. Falling in love again was out of the question. Yet each time she glanced in Blake's direction, her heartbeat accelerated and breathing was something she had to think about and command her body to do.

Unfortunately, she recognized the feeling. Over the last two weeks, she'd fallen in love with Blake.

Her appetite gone, she folded the remains of her sandwich in her napkin. Her voice hardly made a dent in the conversations swirling around them. "Thanks, Blake."

"You're welcome. We gotta keep you fed," he teased. "And I know something else you need. Don't make any plans tonight. I'm taking you somewhere special."

"It's not about the sandwich." Elizabeth took a deep breath and exhaled slowly, trying to find the right words to say. "It's about you being here and doing all this for Jordan."

His gaze shifted past her shoulder as if looking for something that remained out of his reach. "I love her. I never knew it could be like this."

"Like what?" Elizabeth hid her grin as she rested her chin on the palm of her hand, watching him struggle for something to say as he wiped his hand across his face.

"I don't know. I've got these crazy mixed-up feelings inside. I've never felt anything like them before."

Elizabeth's grin became a full-on smile. She'd pretty much felt the same way, even though she'd been terrified when the nurse handed Jordan to her in the hospital room all those years ago. "Like how when you hold her hand, it makes you feel all warm and fuzzy inside and ready to conquer the world? How you would do anything for her? Lay down your life for hers?"

"Yes."

"Welcome to parenthood, Blake. It's the most awesome thing in the world." Something shifted again inside her as she delved into Blake's deep blue eyes. Another piece of wall fell from around her heart.

"Blake Crawford?"

"Yes." Blake pulled his gaze from her and looked at the man a few years younger than them.

Elizabeth did, too, glad for the interruption. Her thoughts had taken a direction she didn't want to follow right now.

"My name's Jason Fletcher. You spoke to me a few days ago? I managed to change my schedule."

Blake shook the stranger's hand, delight erasing the fine lines creasing his forehead. "Jason, welcome. Let me introduce you to Dr. Elizabeth Randall. This is Jordan's mother. Elizabeth, this is Jason. I'll let him tell you who he is."

"Elizabeth, pleased to meet you." The man pulled out a handful of stamped envelopes from a folder he carried and held them in his hands. "I'm your daughter's uncle. Tessa Pruitt was my half sister."

God seemed to be providing miracles today. More joy filled her heart. Elizabeth rose from her chair and clasped his hand in hers. "Hi, Jason. I'm so glad to meet you."

"I didn't believe Blake when he first called me a few days ago. Then while I was going through my mother's things—she passed away last year—I found a few letters. I had no idea I had an older sister. My mom gave her up before I was born and never spoke her name." A stricken look crossed his face. "And I never had a chance to meet her."

"I'm sorry to hear about your mother. My condolences. For Tessa, as well."

Jason shifted on his feet. "Thanks. Anyway, once I discovered the truth, I called Blake back and found out about Jordan's leukemia. I asked him not to tell you until I knew I could make it. Like everyone else, I'm here to be tested."

Tears filled her eyes. She'd become a virtual fountain these past few days—a far cry from the stoic and unflappable Dr. Randall. Yet the feeling was something she could get used to if it meant better days ahead. "That's wonderful. Thank you. You don't know how much this means to me."

"Would it be possible to meet Jordan?"

Elizabeth couldn't ignore the pleading look in his eyes. She couldn't imagine what it would be like to find out about a sister decades later, only to discover she'd passed away and her daughter was gravely ill. Jordan would be ecstatic to find out her extended family had grown by at least one. "Of course. Once we're done here, we'll go to the hospital and I'll introduce you. Right this way." Elizabeth took him to the table where he filled out his paperwork.

Blake watched Elizabeth and Jason. It was good to see her glow with happiness, but Blake wanted to be the one to cause it. Emotion pooled in his gut and if he didn't know better, he'd identify the feeling as jealousy. He had no rights to her, regardless of the fact that she made him want things that contradicted his current outlook on life.

He wasn't meant for marriage. But then again, until he'd received the letter from Tessa, he hadn't been into being a father, either. And yet, fatherhood had been thrust upon him and he seemed to be doing okay—he had Elizabeth to show him how. Maybe with help he could learn to be good husband material after all.

Or maybe not. Eventually, he'd have to come to terms with it, but not in the last fifteen minutes of the drive.

He began to clean up, glad for the physical activity to release the tension within. Maybe Eric would do some more rounds of paintball with him this afternoon. He looked over at the table where Eric still sat with Susie, their heads close together, the beautiful woman laughing at something Eric said. No paintball today, or any day soon.

On autopilot, he continued to clean up and put the tables and chairs away that they were finished using. If he could just expend enough energy to wear himself out, he could forget about the feelings Elizabeth evoked inside him.

"We're here." Blake pulled into one of the last open spots and cut the engine.

"And where would that be?" Elizabeth unbuckled herself and glanced around the resort parking lot filled with cars. They'd driven almost thirty miles into the northern part of the valley to the little town of Cave Creek. Still unclear as to why they were there, she was glad she'd listened to Blake's advice to wear comfortable clothes and shoes. It looked as if they'd be walking a bit.

"The Living Desert Land Trust Symphony is tonight. Matt's wife had tickets for the fundraiser, but she wasn't feeling well, so he gave them to me. We both need a night out, especially after today. Come on. Let's celebrate and have some fun."

Elizabeth wasn't sure about the celebration part just yet, not until they found a match, but having fun sounded like something she needed more of. "A symphony? That doesn't seem to fit you."

"I'm crushed." He gave her his signature grin as he helped her from her seat. "It doesn't, but I'm always willing to try new things. How about you?"

"I'm game, I guess. It doesn't look like I have a choice." She smiled at him, appreciating the way the setting sun cast a glow across his features, softening them. She found herself relaxing for the first time in months.

His hand never left her waist as they followed the signs along the cement path that wound through the casitas and by the golf course. A large eucalyptus towered over a quaint wooden wagon by one of the buildings, and strategically placed flower beds offset the brown gravel and added more color to the lush green grass.

He stopped them beneath a mesquite tree and pointed toward the green. "Look. A coyote."

Elizabeth watched the thin, grayish-white mottled canine trot across the grass. "Now all we need is a roadrunner."

"I'm sure we'll see one of those, too, and I wouldn't be surprised to see a herd of javalinas." He pulled her closer to let a group of other symphony goers pass on the path. Elizabeth allowed him to wrap his arms around her waist as she settled against him and watched the sun set over the mountains. Her actions surprised her. It was as if she'd known Blake for years, not a few weeks. "You know, I was so disappointed when I saw a roadrunner for the first time. It looked nothing like the cartoon. Look, there's one."

"Really?" She watched the long-legged bird pause and raise his long tail feathers as he cocked his head before sprinting off into the brush. "You're right." Her gaze took in the various cacti dotting the landscape along with other native trees and shrubs. "This place is beautiful. I've never really seen much of the Sonoran Desert outside Phoenix or Scottsdale. I need to explore my surroundings more."

"I'd be happy to show you." He released her reluctantly. "Come on. We don't want to miss dinner. I've heard great things about the restaurant that's catering this event."

They walked the rest of the way in silence holding hands, until the path opened up onto the driving range of the golf course where tents, tables and a stage had been set up. People milled about, some dressed in sequins, others in Western-style shirts and jeans. Elizabeth was dressed somewhere in between with her blue silk blouse and tailored tan slacks. She eyed Blake's sport jacket and jeans. No matter what he wore, he looked handsome. Her breath hitched again.

"Let's check in and find our table. Then we can walk around. Looks like there's a silent auction of some sort," he said, and squeezed her hand.

"Works for me." Elizabeth didn't feel like sitting at the table yet, making small talk with a bunch of strangers. At least she'd have Blake at her side, and she found herself looking forward to the rest of the night.

A few moments later, they stood under the big tent perusing the auction donations. She grimaced at the neon picture of a desert landscape. "That's interesting."

"That's not as bad as the picture frame made with pencils and crayons. Look," he whispered in her ear and pointed to the display a few feet over.

"I actually kind of like that." Elizabeth dragged him in front of it. "That gives me an idea of what I can do with all the stuff sitting in plastic bags that Jordan refuses to give up." She pulled out her phone and snapped a picture.

"If you have a glue gun, I can find an old picture frame." They moved on to the next auction for a foursome of golf at the resort. "Do you golf?"

Elizabeth shook her head. If she had four to five hours of free time, she certainly wouldn't be chasing a little white ball around in the grass.

"Me, either. I'd rather be rock climbing or hang gliding." He stared at her intently, a bemused expression on his face. He must have read her thoughts. "Or maybe just taking a long, rambling hike."

Elizabeth shrugged off his gaze and stopped in front of the spa package. "This is more my style." Some pampering would feel really good, but not until they got Jordan well. She shivered as the sun disappeared. Her short sleeves would be no match for the evening temperatures.

"Here." Blake shrugged off his sport jacket and settled it across her shoulders. "I guess I should have suggested a sweater or something. I didn't know we'd be outside."

"Thanks. But won't you be cold?" Elizabeth slipped her arms inside the sleeves, glad for the warmth to cut the slight breeze. She inhaled and took in his lingering scent. What would it feel like to have Blake's arms around her all the time?

"I'll be fine. Looks like it's time for dinner. Shall we?" He held out his arm. Elizabeth laughed as she tucked hers through his and they walked back to their table. This companionship she felt with Blake was new and made her giddy and feel almost childlike again. She liked that feeling.

Dinner was superb and so was the chocolate dessert topped with the flowers from an ocotillo. Their table-mates, various members of the community and the land trust, welcomed them with ease.

As he sat back in his chair and draped his arm across the back of Elizabeth's, Blake couldn't remember a more perfect evening. As part of the festivities, a local bird rescue organization was about to release a mended owl back into the night sky. The scene added another emotional touch as the majestic bird took flight.

"Jordan loves owls. I wish she could have seen that."

"She'll have other opportunities, Elizabeth. I promise." He made a note to talk to the man who'd released the owl. In the meantime, with the music about to start, he didn't want the night to end.

"Mr. Crawford?" A young woman dressed in a sequined shirt and wearing a cowboy hat and boots stopped by the table with a clipboard.

"Yes." He sat up straighter, his heart lurching. Had he won one of the silent auctions? He hadn't really expected to win any when he'd secretly stopped by on his way to get coffee for Elizabeth.

Elizabeth shifted in her seat and stared at him, her eyes dark because of the darkened skies, yet he could see her eyebrows rise.

"Congratulations." She handed him an envelope and a long slender box along with her clipboard. "I just need your signature here."

Once the woman left, Blake's hand shook as he pushed the envelope and box toward Elizabeth. Would she like what he'd won, or would she chastise him for spending the money even if it was for a good cause? His nerves taut, he waited for her reaction. "Here. This is for you, and this is for Jordan."

Elizabeth fingered the long envelope before pulling out the certificate to the spa. Her mouth formed an *O* and a small gasp escaped her lips. When she opened the box and saw the silver necklace with an owl pendant attached, more moisture gathered in the corners of her eyes.

"Thanks, Blake. This is very kind of you. And Jordan will love it." She leaned over and kissed his lips.

Even though the chair didn't move, the tremors he felt reminded him of the earthquake he'd experienced in San Diego last month. It had started slowly, gathered strength and rattled everything around him for a few seconds and then subsided, leaving car alarms blaring and a low buzz of conversations. He liked Elizabeth more than he should.

She pulled back suddenly. "I didn't bid on anything for you."

Blake wrapped his arm around her shoulders and pulled her closer as the strains of violins filled the air. "You didn't need to. You've already given me the best gift possible. My daughter."

"Where are we going?" Jordan piped up from the backseat of Blake's car after church Sunday afternoon.

"A place I used to go when I was a kid." Blake turned into the parking lot and pulled into one of the last vacant spots. Ever since his conversation with Elizabeth at Tillie's, he couldn't get Encanto Park off his mind.

He'd switched shifts to be able to spend the day with Elizabeth and Jordan, but not inside the hospital. Like the doctor had said, his daughter needed fresh air and a different view other than the white walls and constant stream of television.

"Really? This place is that old?" Jordan slipped off her seat and stepped outside into the bright sunshine. She stretched her thin arms over her head as Blake removed the borrowed wheelchair from the back. Jordan could walk, but he'd brought it along so she wouldn't tire from all the exertion. He'd planned a big day of activities, starting with a picnic.

"Older. This park was started in the nineteen-thirties."

"That's ancient, isn't it, Mom?" Jordan settled herself in the chair and allowed Elizabeth to tuck the light blue blanket around her legs. A cool front had blown in overnight, dropping the temperatures, and Blake wanted to make sure she didn't catch a chill.

A smile curved Elizabeth's lips, and Blake wanted to make it permanent. She deserved happiness. They all did. For a brief moment he envisioned a healthy Jordan walking between them, cancer-free and looking forward to all that life had to offer, God willing.

"Ancient? That depends on your point of view. In the big scheme, it's relatively new compared to the Anasazi ruins dotting the area, but to you, anything older than twenty is ancient." She tweaked Jordan's nose and adjusted the red scarf around her head. "Ready?"

"Don't we need the picnic basket?"

"Of course. Here you go." Blake placed the wicker

basket on her lap, closed the hatch and locked his vehicle. "The best spots are by the lagoon. Come on."

Five minutes later, Elizabeth unfolded the woven Mexican blanket and set up their picnic on the grassy area not too far from the water's edge. The spot was just as perfect as he remembered and he was glad he'd chosen to come here instead of the main picnic area.

If he had caught the stares of the other kids as they went by, he knew Jordan had, as well. Cocooned inside the hospital with all the other sick kids had made his daughter feel at least a bit normal. Here, though, the red scarf wrapped around her bald head stood out. So did the wheelchair.

"Mom, can I go down by the water for a few minutes?" Jordan stood and motioned toward the spot where the ducks and geese lazily swam near the shore.

Elizabeth's hands stilled on the bag of potato chips, hesitation creating creases in her forehead. Blake watched her, struggling with the same thoughts. If Jordan had been healthy, it would have been a no-brainer, but they were both afraid to let go. Yet being overprotective wasn't the answer either. Their gazes met and Blake gave her a slight nod and a wink. Everything would be okay.

"Sure. Just don't wander too far. Lunch is almost ready."

"Here, take this." Blake pulled a packet of duck food from the basket and handed it to Jordan. "Just watch out for the geese. They can be mean."

"Thanks, Dad." In Blake's mind, there was no better name in the world.

Blake settled down on the blanket next to Elizabeth and watched the sunlight play against the water's surface and kiss the leaves on the palm trees swaying on the island in the middle of the water. The sunlight and fresh air would do wonders for her. Sounds of laughter carried on the slight breeze and Blake watched Jordan stroll down to the water's edge. Elizabeth tensed beside him. He put his hand on her arm to stop her from going after Jordan. "She'll be fine. Relax. The water's not deep."

Blake moved his hand down until it covered Elizabeth's. When she didn't pull away, his gaze wandered to her face. Some of the tension of the past few weeks had seeped out, replaced by what he perceived as contentment. He found himself wanting to know more about the woman who'd raised his child. "Why did you adopt Jordan?"

Blake didn't let her pull her hand away because he liked the feel of it underneath his. He could get used to spending more of his downtime with her and Jordan instead of doing those crazy, adrenaline pumping activities that really left him with no satisfaction once the money cleared from his account.

"Lunch is ready, don't you think we should call her?" Elizabeth felt the blood leave her face. Jordan's adoption was not what she wanted to talk about. Guilt singed her thoughts and the last thing she wanted to think about was the day she talked Tessa into giving Elizabeth her unborn child.

"Lunch can wait a bit—there's nothing that will spoil. I should know. I packed it."

Jordan's laughter floated in the air around them as Elizabeth stalled, trying to form some sort of answer. What could she tell him that didn't make her sound manipulative or downright selfish and greedy? That she put her own needs over that of her former roommate who had come to her in tears, desperate to figure out how to tell her parents?

Elizabeth hadn't really helped her old roommate find a solution so much as an answer to her own prayers. Would Tessa have given in so easily if Elizabeth hadn't suggested the adoption?

Elizabeth had put in another call to her attorney last week and still no response. Elizabeth had always suspected that something would go wrong with the adoption. And it had, but in a different way. Never in a million years had she ever suspected she'd be in a park with Jordan's biological father, hopelessly falling in love with him. "I don't think you really want to know."

"I do." He wove his fingers through hers and pulled them to his chest. More guilt shredded her composure as she relived the memories buried deep within her.

Had she made the right decision? She thought she had, but lately she wasn't so sure. Blake deserved to know the truth. At least then she could move forward. She hung her head in shame and her words came out in a whisper, barely distinguishable from the slight breeze. "It's actually very selfish on my part."

"Try me." Blake lifted his fingers to her chin and tilted her head so she had no choice but to look at him. She couldn't make out his eyes behind his sunglasses.

She exhaled slowly, gathering courage. "Tom was

sterile. I knew that going into our marriage. I wanted kids. He did, too." Moisture gathered in her eyes. "One night Tessa called me in tears, begging me to meet her. I hadn't seen her in almost six months, but I told her to come over. When she arrived, I knew it was something bad. She looked scared."

"If she was pregnant, that would make sense. Her parents would have disowned her if they found out."

Elizabeth nodded and shuddered. "She didn't say so in those words, but I figured that out quickly. Like I'd said, I'd never met them, nor had I ever talked to them until a few days ago." Elizabeth swallowed hard. "When Tessa told me she was pregnant, I was the one that suggested adoption. I saw an opportunity and grabbed it. My chance to have a family without going through the stress of using an adoption agency. It didn't matter that the unborn baby wasn't ours. We loved her. But Tessa told us she didn't know who the father was and never mentioned her marriage. Tom and I both thought she was alone."

"And she was. It wasn't a real marriage. Not like it should have been. It was two people who weren't meant for each other, living together and creating another life that neither one was ready for. My guess is by the time Tessa started showing, I was already in the military ready to go overseas. She had no idea where I was because I wanted it that way. If the roles had been reversed, I would have done the same thing."

"No wonder she jumped at my offer. I'm still sorry, Blake."

"Sorry for what?" He must have missed something.

"That I took Jordan away from you. I should have insisted Tessa find the father and give him the opportunity to make the decision himself. Not that I wouldn't jump at the chance to adopt her all over again."

"You have nothing to be sorry for, so quit beating yourself up." Blake kissed each knuckle, then planted another kiss on her palm. "Tessa made the right choice. You've done a wonderful job."

Elizabeth graced him with one of her smiles, relieved to finally have that off her chest. She'd never even told Tom the whole truth. "You're not so bad yourself. Even though it's scary, parenting is more instinctive than people realize."

"Some people choose to ignore their instincts, I guess."

Elizabeth knew he was referring to his father. In her dealings with Dr. Crawford, he'd never struck her that way, but she hadn't lived with him. "Some people are fools."

"Did you go with Tessa for her appointments?"

Nodding, Elizabeth wished she could convey all the emotions and feelings of that time, but words couldn't do them justice. "As much as I could with my schedule. I did get to see one of Tessa's ultrasounds and listen to Jordan's heartbeat. It was incredible and made it so much more real for us. And we were there when Jordan was born. I was so scared when the nurse placed her in my arms. Here was a new life and I was responsible for her for better or worse. I thought Tessa was going to change her mind, but she didn't."

He leaned in closer. "Do you think you'll ever marry again?"

His words took her breath away. She blinked and struggled to answer. "I doubt it. It was too painful losing Tom. How about you?"

Blake leaned in, tilted his head and touched her lips with his. "My head tells me I didn't get it right the first time, but my heart has other ideas."

"Hey, Mom, Dad, look at this." Jordan called from the edge of the lake.

Elizabeth scooted back on the blanket and away from Blake. That was all Jordan needed to see—she'd be planning their wedding in no time. "Look at what?"

"This." Jordan leaned over and held out her hand. Five ducks started to eat food from her palm, while others approached from the lake. Her laughter filled the air again.

Elizabeth would never get tired of that sound. "I haven't heard Jordan laugh like that in a long time. Thanks for doing this."

"My pleasure."

Blake sat back on the blanket and stared at his daughter feeding the ducks by the lake. Elizabeth had shown him the photos and told him the stories, yet there was so much he'd missed by not being there. All that time could never be replaced, because he hadn't been there for Tessa or Elizabeth or Jordan. In his own way, he'd become his father. No more. Staring up at the sky, he praised God that he'd been brought into Jordan's life from this point forward. He'd never take anything for granted again, and that included the woman beside him who had let him into her daughter's life, and into hers, as well.

Chapter Twelve

"Daddy, please?" Jordan tugged at Blake's shirt after they'd cleaned up lunch and gathered their belongings. "Can't we try it just this once?"

"Sounds like fun." His gaze found Elizabeth, her lip trapped between her teeth.

"A pedal boat ride?" She stared at the dock half full of blue four-seat boats sitting in the murky green water. Tension created havoc in her stomach. "Not me. I can't swim."

"You can't? Why?"

Elizabeth balled her hands. Just the idea of going out on the wide expanse of water made it difficult for her to breathe. Having Jordan at the edge of the lake earlier had been one thing—going out into the middle was something else. If something happened to both of them, Elizabeth wouldn't be able to save them. "My parents thought studying was more important. I'm probably the only adult in Phoenix who can't."

"There are others, trust me. Does Jordan know how?"

"Yes."

"We'll just go out for a bit and I'll do all the paddling. It'll be fine. I promise. I won't let anything happen to our daughter." He recognized her fears, which made her feel a tiny bit better. So did the reassuring touch on her arm. "It's only ten feet deep at the most and Jordan will wear a life jacket."

"Please, Mom?" The pleading look on Jordan's face did her in. She had to learn to let go. Besides, Jordan and Blake should have some quality time together.

"Have fun, then. I'll be waiting right here." Elizabeth pulled out the blanket and settled herself down near the edge of the water.

As promised, Blake did all the paddling. Jordan weighed next to nothing and the small boat tilted slightly. Still, the pure delight on her face made it all worthwhile as they tooled around the lake.

An exhausted Jordan fell asleep immediately as soon as she lay down on the blanket next to Elizabeth. Blake was doubly glad he'd brought the wheelchair now. He actually ached himself. They'd done the train ride and the parachute ride and they'd been on the merry-go-round five times, but the pedal boat had done him in. He glanced at his daughter. Color infused Jordan's cheeks and pure contentment overrode the peaked expression she'd worn when they'd come to the park a few hours ago.

He wouldn't change a thing.

"This was such a great idea." Elizabeth spoke softly as she ran her fingers up and down Jordan's arm. "Thanks for bringing us here."

"This park is one of the happy memories. Today doubly so."

Blake tilted his head back and pulled in a long breath. A man-made oasis in the heart of the city. Man-made, but God had stamped His mark on it. He leaned over and sneaked another kiss from Elizabeth while Jordan slept.

"We have a match from an anonymous donor." Dr. Pearson pulled his glasses from his face and gave them a half smile. It was a little over a week after the donor drive.

"Praise the Lord." She reached out and grabbed Blake's hand. The action felt as natural now as breathing.

"So what kind of time line are we looking at now?"

Dr. Pearson leaned forward. "One to two weeks."

"One to two weeks? Why so long?"

Beside Elizabeth, Blake shifted in his chair. Any second now, she'd see his hand push through the short stubble on his head. She wasn't disappointed. Finally, Blake pulled his arm from her hand and stood.

As a man of action, Blake was used to getting things done quickly and efficiently. Elizabeth knew this was killing him as much as it was her. Yet she continued to have the faith that God would cure her daughter if it was His will. Blake seemed to still be struggling with that.

"Jordan has to be well enough to go through a final round of chemo to kill everything off so the transplant will work."

"Well enough?" Blake ground out the words.

"Her counts have to be at a certain level. They're not

there right now. But we're close." Dr. Pearson closed the folder. "I'm glad you took her to the park last weekend. The outing did her good."

"Thanks, Jim." Elizabeth stared at Blake and swallowed her rising panic, sensing the words the doctor didn't say.

They were almost out of time.

As a doctor, she knew that. As a mother, she refused to believe it. *Please, Lord, heal Jordan.* She shot out of her seat, knowing that she could lean on Blake. Darkness crept into her line of vision and Elizabeth's knees threatened to buckle under her weight as she stumbled to the door.

"We'll get through this, Elizabeth." Outside in the hall, he pulled her to him and cradled her in his arms. She released all the tears that had built since she'd first learned of Jordan's illness.

Blake's tears mingled with hers as she gulped for air and composure. She had to be strong, stay strong for Jordan's sake. But because the dam had been broken, she wasn't able to put her emotions back into the compartment relegated for them. Especially when Blake's lips briefly found hers.

His hand came up and touched her cheek, removing any doubt that the kiss had been a random act of kindness. Despite her reservations, she knew there was something behind it. They both felt it, even though they tried to distance themselves from the feeling.

She closed her eyes, trying to regain her composure and find Dr. Randall. "I need to get back to the E.R. I'll see you later, Blake."

* * *

"Dr. Randall." Elizabeth answered her phone later that day as she waited at the station for a patient to come in.

"Hi, Dr. Randall, this is Kerrie Maxwell returning your call."

The adoption attorney.

Elizabeth's heart pounded with dread. Pushing away from the wall, she felt the blood drain from her face as she lifted her hand to her forehead. After all this time, she'd almost forgotten about her call.

"Hi, Kerrie. Thanks for calling back."

Elizabeth motioned to Lidia she was taking a quick break.

"Sorry, I was in Europe on my honeymoon for a few weeks. My *former* assistant dropped the ball on returning my calls to let my clients know it would be a short while before I could get back to them." Kerrie continued. "I'd like you to stop by my office so we can discuss your case in person."

Elizabeth's agitation mounted. She swallowed, the words barely making their way past her constricted throat. "I can be there at five-thirty tonight if that works for you."

Elizabeth pulled up outside the stucco building and switched off the ignition at 5:25 p.m. Her nails dug into her palms as she sat in the driver's seat, a million scenarios crowding out other thoughts, and none of them good. Fuchsia bougainvilleas graced the front walls and multicolored lantana lined the sidewalk leading up to the blue front door. The place looked the same to Elizabeth as it had almost ten years earlier.

A few moments passed as Elizabeth's eyes adjusted to the interior. The first thing she noticed was the large fish tank separating the waiting room from the empty reception desk. The second was Blake, sitting in a chair next to the water cooler. The bottom of her world fell out.

His being here could mean only one thing.

"Blake?" Fighting to grab a breath, Elizabeth acknowledged him as she walked to the fish tank and stared blankly at a blue fish with a yellow tail swimming lazily among the bright coral. They were so close to a cure for Jordan. And yet she was about to lose her in a different way, just as she'd feared.

No. Jordan was her daughter. The attorney was simply going to confirm that, which explained Blake's presence.

Out of the corner of her eye, through the glass, she watched Blake stand and approach her. His hand made its way to his shaved head only to drop back down to his side. He moved in beside her and stared at the tank, as well. "Elizabeth."

"What are you doing here?" Watching the fish swim lazily around would have calmed her if Blake hadn't been there. But she supposed he had every right as Jordan's father.

"I was asked to come. And you?"

Elizabeth floundered, afraid to vocalize the reason for the visit. "I—I called the attorney when you first showed up."

"Why?" Gently he turned her face so she had no choice but to look into his eyes. The love she saw behind his questioning expression frightened her even more.

"To see if the adoption was legal."

"You think—" Blake dropped his hand from her face and stepped away from her, distrust and disgust mingling in his expression.

"Put yourself in my shoes. I was afraid."

"Afraid that I would take her away from you?" His eyes widened and his mouth dropped open as a flush spead across his face.

Elizabeth looked away and nodded.

"Hello. Glad you both could make it." The tall, thin, dark-haired woman in her mid-forties approached from the hallway behind them.

"Thanks for seeing me. Us."

"No problem. I'll always do follow-up on any of my cases." Kerrie shook Elizabeth's hand. "And you must be Jordan's biological father, Blake Crawford." Kerrie spoke in a no-nonsense tone. "Kerrie Maxwell. Pleased to meet you." She shook his hand, as well. "Right this way, please."

Once inside of the attorney's office, Elizabeth noticed that the back wall was now filled with more pictures of babies and children than when she and Tom had been here. Photos of all the successful adoptions Kerrie had done. Elizabeth's gaze roamed over the hundreds of photos searching for the one she'd given Kerrie days after Jordan's adoption.

Where was it? Tension tightened her neck muscles

and dread pulsed through her veins, creating an instant headache. Elizabeth massaged her temples, but the throbbing only increased. Only Kerrie's positive analysis of the situation could eradicate the pounding.

"Please sit down." Kerrie ushered them into two matching leather chairs before she took her own seat behind the massive wood desk and retrieved a legal-sized folder. She glanced at it briefly before she closed it and pulled her reading glasses off her nose. "I'm sorry to hear about Jordan's illness."

"Thanks." Both Elizabeth and Blake spoke together.

"When I spoke to you on the phone, I didn't tell you why I wanted you here, Blake. I will now. Elizabeth had concerns about whether her daughter's adoption was legal."

"I'm aware of that now." Out of the corner of her eye she saw his grip tighten on the armrests. "She needn't have worried. She's got—we've got too many other things to be concerned with."

Kerrie's fingers played with the pen in her hand. "When Tessa first came into my office, she stated she didn't know who the father was." Opening the folder again, she pulled out a few sheets of paper and placed them on top. "For whatever reason, she lied. I did some checking and pulled your marriage and divorce papers."

Elizabeth pulled at her collar. Her tension increased as they waited for the attorney to continue.

"Blake and Tessa Crawford were divorced at the time the paperwork was signed. According to the laws of this state, the adoption wasn't legal because Blake didn't sign off on it. I'm sorry, Elizabeth. Jordan Randall legally belongs to Blake."

Elizabeth almost collapsed out of her chair. Her hands gripped the wood arms to keep her from sliding to the floor. Jordan wasn't hers. And the worst thing about the whole situation was she'd brought it on herself. Tears spilled down her cheeks and the more she tried to wipe them away, the harder they fell.

"What?" Blake jumped out of his seat, his eyes widening. Jordan belonged to him? How could that be?

"Custody will revert immediately unless you sign the adoption papers." Kerrie pushed a stack of papers across her desk toward Blake.

"There's no other way?"

"I can think of one, but it would involve a member of the clergy or a justice of the peace."

Marriage. Out of the question. Blake flexed his hands and stared at the ink on the white paper. Leaning over the desk, he picked up a pen. The words in front of him blended together into a mass of black. Custody should belong to Elizabeth. Elizabeth was a great parent. She truly did love Jordan.

But his love for Jordan grew inside him, stabbing and twisting in his gut.

Stricken, he stared at the pen in a hand he had a hard time recognizing as his own. If he signed the paperwork, he was giving his daughter away. Again. If he didn't sign, then he was ripping Jordan from the only home she'd ever known.

His other choice was to marry Elizabeth and create the family Jordan wanted.

The four walls crashed in around him, making it hard to breathe. He had to escape. Flinging the pen down on the desk, he backed away toward the door. "I need some time to think."

Sleep had eluded Blake all night and he was struggling to keep his eyes open today. What should he do? The easiest thing would be to marry the doctor and start over again. He couldn't deny that he'd fallen in love with her, but the whole dad thing was new to him, and being a husband again—when he was such a lousy one the first time around—didn't make much sense either.

Besides, what if Elizabeth said no? A few kisses did not make a marriage. Marriage took love, commitment, respect and a whole multitude of things.

And could he handle living with a doctor again?

"House fire. Let's go." Matt broke into Blake's thoughts. He had it bad if he hadn't even heard the alarm. Donning his gear, he slipped into the ambulance on the passenger side. Corey took one look at him and took the driver's seat.

"Are you sure you should even be at work right now?"

"Positive." He needed something to occupy his mind. "I'm just not sure I should drive, that's all."

Corey whistled, flipped on the siren and pulled out after the fire truck. "Okay, but be careful today. You're not yourself right now."

Blake knew as soon as he entered the burning building he'd made a mistake. Not only had he put himself in jeopardy, but he'd put his coworkers in danger, too. Heat pierced his skin despite his protective gear. Stucco houses went up fast. Sweat poured down his face. He wasn't invincible. This adrenaline rush might be the one he didn't walk away from.

He'd gone back into the burning house for a girl named Belle on the word of a child. He should have checked with the woman holding her hand, but the little girl's eyes reminded him of his daughter. The one he'd been thinking about all night and day. He hadn't been able to refuse the little girl's plea any more than he could refuse his daughter. Stupid. Not only that, he'd disobeyed a direct order from his captain. There'd be a huge consequence to pay when—or if—he got out.

Images of Elizabeth and Jordan rose in his mind's eye—the doctor wearing a genuine grin as they picnicked at Encanto Park, the sun kissing her delicate features and highlighting the flecks of gold in her blue eyes, Jordan at the impromptu Boston Brothers concert, her problems forgotten for a brief moment in time.

He might never see them again.

Love for both of them pierced his heart again.

And yet his daughter's future was still uncertain. There was a multitude of things that could go wrong.

If she didn't make it, Blake wasn't sure Elizabeth's feelings for him, if she had any, would survive. His own father had rejected him. So had Tessa when she hadn't even tried to contact him when she discovered her pregnancy. Suddenly he was afraid Elizabeth would do the same.

Old insecurities blotted out all the goodness that had

transpired in his life lately. He wasn't good enough. He'd never been good enough and never would be.

Nonsense. He was good enough.

His father had just never seen it in his preoccupation with work. But Elizabeth saw it. So did Jordan.

Blake had to get out and get back to the people he loved.

A gray fog tried to descend over him, cocooning him in its death grip. Ice chilled his blood. His heart raced in panic, the pounding reverberating in his entire being. He fought for calm as smoke filled his vision.

He dropped to a crawl. Disoriented because he'd let down his guard and hadn't paid attention to his surroundings when he ran in, he flailed around, trying to find a way out.

He knew he needed help.

And not just any help.

God was the only one who could help him now—his coworkers would be bigger fools if they came inside after him. Drawing in a deep breath, he paused and bowed his head. Instinctively his hands came together. Blake didn't beg or plead or make any promises; he simply spoke what was in his heart. "Lord, please help me. I need You."

A renewed sense of urgency and strength clutched him in its grasp. He continued to crawl down the hall away from the flames threatening to burn him alive. A sliver of light caught his eye down the hall to his left.

His fingers found a strip of molding and then an indent. A door. This should hopefully lead to the front bedroom and freedom. He found the knob, his gloved fingers slipping three times before he finally managed to get it to open.

Just on the other side, he leaned back and gasped for more oxygen from his tank. *Thank You, Lord.*

The room had yet to fill with smoke. He glanced around the pink-and-purple princess room. Not a child in sight. He crawled to the bed and pulled up the fabric. Nothing. The closet held only clothes and shoes. When something shot past him, he turned around. Hovering by the window, he spied a little black-and-white kitten, mewing frantically.

Belle was a cat? Blake crawled toward the cat and the window, and hopefully freedom.

Chapter Thirteen

"Okay, Nicholas, you're going to be just fine." Elizabeth put down the metal detector and ruffled the toddler's brown hair. "Next time, the penny goes into the bank, not in your mouth. You gave your mom quite a scare, you know."

Nicholas nodded at her, his hazel eyes wide. He popped his thumb out of his mouth. "'Kay. I go now?"

"Of course." She smiled as she picked up the small boy and placed him in his mother's arms. "My own daughter did the same thing at about his age, Mrs. Pratt." Pain radiated from her heart. The child she'd raised since birth was not technically her daughter. Not until Blake signed the paperwork. And from the look on his face yesterday, that wasn't going to happen.

Focus on work.

She looked at the mother again. "The penny should pass in a day or two. If he experiences stomach pain or vomiting, bring him back here immediately."

The dark-haired woman looked at her gratefully. "So he'll be okay?"

"He will. It happens more often than you think." Elizabeth ruffled the boy's hair again. "Remember what I said. Pennies go in the bank. Food goes in the mouth."

A few minutes later she stood at the nurses' station, staring at the clock behind Lidia's head. The minutes dragged by, the seconds barely moving. Even a pot of water boiled faster. Lunchtime. Jordan would be eating upstairs. Elizabeth wanted to go to her, but couldn't sneak away—a multi-car accident occupied the rest of her coworkers. The limbo was killing her. She should have left everything alone.

"Dr. Randall?" Lidia broke into her thoughts. "Incoming patient—a fireman down with smoke inhalation. No one else is available—will you take him?"

"A fireman?" She had no idea if Blake was working today, because they hadn't spoken after he'd left Kerrie's office. Her heart leaped to her throat and her mind filled with scenarios, each one worse than the one before.

Snapping on a fresh set of gloves, Elizabeth met the stretcher in the middle of the room. Cotton filled her mouth and her knees knocked until she thought she'd lose her balance.

Soot streaked Blake's pale face as he lay there, unconscious with an oxygen mask covering his nose and mouth.

Elizabeth grabbed his coworker by the arm. "What happened?"

Corey wiped his streaked face with his sleeve. "He went back inside a burning house to save a child, though it ended up being a kitten. The roof collapsed on him and dislodged his breathing apparatus. We got him out as quickly as we could, but he'd already been in there for a few minutes."

All medical knowledge disappeared from Elizabeth's brain. Her mouth opened and shut, but no orders came out. Not again. Never again. She loved Blake, but she couldn't go through losing someone again.

"Dr. Randall, should we intubate him?" the nurse questioned while an intern hovered beside her.

"I don't know. Blake? Can you hear me?" Desperation laced her voice. The entire engine company milled around in the background, staring at her. So did her co-workers. The unflappable Dr. Randall had finally lost it. If she hadn't been so distraught, the irony might have made her laugh. Blood drained from her head and left her dizzy and disoriented. She forced her lungs to take in oxygen while she stared at the man she loved. A sob rose in her throat.

"Dr. Randall. Dr. Randall?"

Elizabeth remained motionless, her fists clenched at her sides, her bottom lip caught between her teeth as she stared down at Blake. It took all her will not to sink to the floor in a pile of tears.

"Dr. Randall?" A hand waved in front of her face. She didn't blink. "Relieved of duty. Please remove yourself from the floor." Dr. Westfall's commanding voice finally sank into her brain.

Forced into retreat, Elizabeth paced the area around the main counter. Dr. Westfall was more than competent and would take care of Blake. Better than she could, apparently. Feeling useless and out of sorts, she signaled her intent to the shocked head nurse and escaped to the cafeteria.

Cup of coffee in hand, she sank onto the chair and mindlessly stirred packet after packet of sugar into her drink. Life went on as usual around her, yet Elizabeth couldn't connect. Her fingers trembled as she leaned her elbow against the table, made a fist and rested her forehead against it. She'd just made a huge mistake.

All because she'd let her emotions get in the way of her work.

Maybe it was time to leave the E.R.

"Mind if I join you?" Dr. Westfall pulled out the chair across from her about thirty minutes later.

"Not at all." The words spilled from her lips, despite the fact she wanted to nurse her wounds in private. She needed time to collect her emotions and put them away in the area reserved for things like that. She made unemotional split-second decisions all the time, yet when it concerned someone close to her, she was useless.

"What happened back there?" Concern and wisdom was etched in each line on the older doctor's face.

"I don't know. I mean, I was fine until I saw who it was. I froze up, couldn't react, couldn't think." Elizabeth sighed. "I've lost my edge."

"No, you haven't. You're one of our best. Take it from me, treating someone you care about is enough to make anyone hesitate. I'm not sure I could have done it, either. I've been fortunate not to have that happen. He's going to be okay, Elizabeth."

"Of course he is, thanks to you. What's his status?"

"It's not as bad as it could have been. He's sedated right now, but he's going to be waking up with a huge headache." He smiled. "Finish your drink and report back to duty."

"Can I see him?"

"He's been transferred to the second floor. By the time you get off work today, he should be a little more coherent."

She gave him a grateful smile and took a sip of her drink. Blake would recover, but Elizabeth would never be the same again.

"Everything okay, Mom?" Jordan's voice filtered into Elizabeth's thoughts.

Mom. That word ripped her world apart again. She wasn't Jordan's mother. Not until Blake signed the paperwork. But at least hearing Jordan say it stopped the instant replay of her reaction in the E.R. this afternoon. Like a bad staph infection, it just kept surfacing no matter how she tried to eradicate it. Peeking inside Blake's hospital room and seeing him lying so still in the bed hadn't helped either.

"Yes, fine." Holding her breath, Elizabeth tried to quiet the butterflies in her stomach, wondering just how much she should tell Jordan. What she really wanted to do was pack up all Jordan's things and just go back to their condo, but she couldn't. Not anymore. Tears hit the back of her eyes. Elizabeth sat down on Jordan's bed and picked up her slender hand.

Jordan was about to start her last round of chemo before the transplant.

Taking her out of the hospital would be a certain death sentence.

They were so close. Elizabeth had to remain strong. They would beat the leukemia and she and Blake would work things out.

"Mom?"

Elizabeth took a deep breath. "Your father was hurt today in a fire. He's going to be okay, though, so don't worry."

"Do we need to say a prayer for him? Have you seen him? Is he really okay? Or will I lose him, too?" Jordan's face paled even further and tears filled her eyes.

Had Elizabeth been that transparent? She had no idea Jordan shared her fears. Her daughter had been so young when Tom died, Elizabeth had been certain she didn't remember the loss. Maybe she was wrong.

What else didn't she know about her daughter? She'd spent so much time working and striving to be the best doctor she could, and trying to be both parents, that she must have missed something. But Blake was a natural father and apparently a better parent than Elizabeth—he was the one who arranged concerts and picnics. Maybe this was the way things were supposed to work out.

She stroked the soft skin on Jordan's face. "He's going to be fine. Just a bit of smoke inhalation."

"Can I see him?" Jordan reached for the scarf to cover her bald head.

"Not right now. He isn't awake yet. Soon." In that moment, Elizabeth decided that she would spend more time with Jordan when she got out of the hospital, regardless of Blake's decision to sign or not. Blake wouldn't deny her time with Jordan, would he? Besides, right after the transplant, someone had to be available to take care of Jordan full-time. "I've decided I'm going to take some time off work."

"So you can take care of both of us when we get out of here? We'd be like a real family."

And that was the crux of Elizabeth's problem. The smoke inhalation wouldn't kill Blake, but the next fire might. But denying that she loved him wasn't the answer either.

Was she ready to take another chance?

"Is that what you really want?"

Jordan nodded.

Maybe they should consider Kerrie's suggestion. At least one person would be happy.

Blake came to with a major headache and a sore throat. His lungs burned and his eyes felt scratchy when he opened his lids. White walls, a TV and the smell of antiseptic assaulted his senses while an IV pinched in his arm.

Good job, Crawford, you've landed yourself in the hospital.

He turned his head toward the window to see darkness pushing out the last remnants of day. The house fire had been around noon, so he'd been out for a while.

"It's about time you woke up." His buddy Eric spoke from the chair to the left of the bed.

"Just wanted to catch up on my sleep." Even talking hurt.

"There are safer ways to do that."

Blake grimaced. "Tell me about it. Guess doctors aren't the only ones who think they're God."

"Far from it. But there's only one God and you're lucky He was with you today."

"He was." Blake rubbed his eyes, the sandpaper sensation making him stop before he'd satisfied the itch. A fit of coughing took him by surprise and more pain racked his body. "What happened? I don't remember."

"You went inside a burning building for someone named Belle. A kitten, Crawford. You went in after a kitten. The roof collapsed, dislodging your equipment, and you got smoke inhalation. Luckily, no one else was injured rescuing you."

Blake glanced around the darkening room. "Where are all the guys?"

His friend gave him a scowl. "Back at the station where you should be. I'm supposed to call them now that you've come to."

"Guess I'll be suspended for a few days. Did the cat make it out?"

A forced chuckle erupted from Eric's lips. "Yes. Since when did you start caring more about other things than your sorry hide?"

Blake stifled a painful yawn. "Since I met my daughter. Does she know?"

"Not sure, but Elizabeth does." Eric leaned forward and rested his elbows on his knees, his look grim. "All the other doctors were attending accident victims when you came in. Despite the fact she's a children's physician, she was your attending."

Blake knew there was more to the story than Eric let on. "What aren't you telling me?"

Eric took his sweet time before he answered. "She lost it, Crawford. Just stood there, white-faced, staring down at you as if she'd seen a ghost. No one knew what to do until Dr. Westfall ordered her off the floor and started barking orders."

Not good. Elizabeth had jeopardized her job because of his actions. "Obviously everyone knows, if you're here."

"You know the rumor mills here. Nothing is secret. Why did you do it?"

"Because—because…" Blake grasped for an answer. How could he respond when he didn't know himself? He searched deep inside and finally acknowledged the sore that had been festering since the day he'd found out he wasn't compatible. "I can't save my own child. I thought the least I could do was save someone else's."

"You don't have to be a bone marrow donor to save Jordan. All you have to do is be there for her. I think you've got your priorities mixed up. Haven't you learned anything from this experience?"

Blake ran a hand across his face, almost dislodging the oxygen tubes in his nose. "Sure. I'm still the same self-centered, uncaring jerk who doesn't deserve to have a daughter."

"But you have been there." A dawning light of comprehension lit Eric's eyes. "This is about your dad, isn't it?"

Blake refused to meet Eric's gaze. Pain squeezed his heart until he thought it would stop beating.

"Listen," Eric said. "Your dad was messed up. Everyone knows he wasn't the same after your mom died, but you're not your father. Sure, he made mistakes. We all do. It's what we learn from them that's important. Even he learned at the end."

Blake bit back a sarcastic laugh. "What did he learn?"

"Look, you probably need to hear this. Despite what you think, your dad was proud of you. I know because he used to come to me to find out how you were doing. In the end, he finally admitted that he'd followed in his father's footsteps and become a doctor because he didn't have the strength to tell the old man no. You had the courage to do your own thing. Too bad he died before he had a chance to tell you."

"Right. And pigs fly."

"I never told you because I didn't think you were ready to hear. I can see you're still not, so believe what you like, but it's the truth. Take a good look in the mirror, and while you're at it, look at what's on the inside as well and start praying for forgiveness." Eric glanced at his watch. "I've gotta run. I'm meeting Susie for a late dinner."

Blake was only too glad to change the subject. "Susie? Elizabeth's friend?"

"Yeah, sometimes the best things are right under our noses but we're too busy doing other things to notice. Think about that next time you do something stupid." Eric stood and strode from the room.

Stupid. Yep. Going back into the burning building had been stupid, no matter what the reason. And he'd hurt Elizabeth in the process. His heart hurt just as much as his body.

Elizabeth had been unable to handle seeing him unconscious, Eric said. Did that mean she loved him?

He loved her. Somehow she'd gotten under his skin. He'd be a fool if he didn't do something about it.

Eric was right. He wasn't his father and he had the power to change things. Blake had been given a gift and suddenly he knew what God wanted him to do.

"Okay, Lord, I get it. Thank You."

He couldn't wait another moment. After pulling the IV from his arm and the oxygen tubes from his nose, he flung the white sheet from his legs and swung them to the floor.

"Where are you going?" Elizabeth's voice cut through his thoughts.

"To see you and Jordan. I have some explaining to do." A cough racked Blake's body as he leaned against the bed, looking only marginally better than when his coworkers had brought him in.

"Who discharged you? Or did you just decide to leave?" Shoving all personal matters aside, Elizabeth grabbed him around his waist before he pitched headfirst onto the floor. "Get back in bed, Blake."

"No."

"Yes." They sounded like children.

"No." He wrapped his arms around her waist and dragged her with him until they leaned against the wall.

The action caused another round of coughing. Concern flared inside her. He shouldn't be exerting himself. She struggled to extricate herself, but despite his injuries, his grip was too strong. "What are you doing?"

"What I've been wanting to do again for days." Blake's lips found hers, but her fears rose to the surface again. What was she doing?

She tried to push him away again. "Stop it, Blake. You're hurt. Obviously the smoke inhalation has affected your brain. How long were you without oxygen?"

He refused to let her go and pulled her closer again. "Not long enough to forget what I want and how to get it."

"What is it you want?"

Blake stilled a moment and looked her straight in the eye. "I don't want to sign the adoption paperwork, and I don't want you to lose her, either. I think Kerrie had the right idea. I want to be a part of a family again. I love you, Elizabeth. Will you marry me?"

Her breath caught in her throat as she stared at Blake. She loved him, too, but her fears paralyzed her. Could she handle it every time Blake went on a call? She didn't know.

"Please don't reject me, Elizabeth. You know it's the best thing for us to do. It's okay if you don't love me. Do it for Jordan." Blake's voice shook. Panic rose in his eyes and his grip on her tightened.

"I'm not rejecting you."

"Than why aren't you answering me? I'll say it again. I love you, Elizabeth, in case you haven't figured it out. Do I need to shout it out on the loudspeaker so everyone knows what's in my heart? I want us to be a family. I'm willing to do what it takes."

But was Elizabeth willing? Did she want to spend the rest of her life afraid of loving again? Tears filled her eyes. That was not God's intended plan for her—she knew it in her heart.

There were no guarantees in life—accidents and sickness happened. So she'd better learn to enjoy it while she could. "I love you, too, Blake Crawford, and the answer is yes. But if you ever do anything so stupid, so idiotic, so—"

He silenced her with another kiss.

"Does this mean I finally get to be a bridesmaid?" Jordan piped up from behind them.

Elizabeth twisted around and saw her daughter standing on the threshold with Rebecca at her side. A huge grin split Jordan's lips and joy filled her. Jordan's prayer had been answered and God was smiling down on them.

"I think it does." Elizabeth and Blake sealed the promise with another long kiss.

Epilogue

"**Y**ou look beautiful, Mom. Are you ready?" Jordan smoothed out the fabric of Elizabeth's cream-colored wedding dress in the back room of the church.

"Yes." Elizabeth stared into the mirror and adjusted one of the flowers tucked into her chin-length hair. This new look still seemed foreign, but in a good way. Like the long, dark, wavy wig on Jordan's head. Six months into remission her hair had grown back, but her daughter had wanted to look exceptional for her parents' marriage. Especially in her dual role as flower girl and aisle escort—she was giving her mom away.

Marriage.

Tears filled her eyes and she grabbed a tissue. Exactly one year ago today, Elizabeth had received word that Jordan's leukemia had come out of remission. And now she was getting married to Jordan's father. Her world was complete.

"Why are you crying, Mom?"

"Because I'm happy. Like I told you before, some people cry when they're happy."

"Oh. I get it now." Jordan smiled at her.

"Ready to go?" Susie glanced at the clock on the wall. "It's time."

Elizabeth nodded and picked up her bouquet, joy filling her heart. Never in a million years had she figured she'd be blessed to find another man to share her life with until one handsome fireman came into her world.

Blake stared at both his girls as they stood at the threshold of the sanctuary. Elizabeth looked more beautiful than ever. Happiness and pride filled him. All he needed was the love of a good woman, his daughter and the ability to be the best dad he could be.

He shifted on his feet as he watched Jordan and Elizabeth walk down the aisle together. But he wasn't uncomfortable—far from it. He was looking forward to spending the rest of his life with his wife and child. And any other child God decided to bless them with. Love welled inside him.

His gaze met Eric's and a grin leaped to his lips. Unlike with his first marriage, he knew what he was getting into and he relished the idea. This time around he had his eyes and heart open, and God sitting with them in the jump seat.

Elizabeth wouldn't have to face any more problems alone and he could be the father he was meant to be. They were about to make a bond that would tie them together in the eyes of God, the church and the state.

The three of them. Together. As it should be.

* * * * *

Dear Reader,

Cancer. I shudder every time I hear that word, yet these days it's almost as common as breathing. Every time I turn around, I know someone who knows someone with the disease. As the mother of two young children, I can't even begin to comprehend what it would be like to have a child with cancer and my heart breaks for those of you readers who do. I pray daily that God helps us find a cure.

Writing *And Father Makes Three* gave me the opportunity to explore the complex subject of bone marrow transplants. The stories and testimonials were truly inspirational and humbling at the same time. A portion of the proceeds of this book will be donated to the Be the Match program to defray the costs associated with the testing. (http://www.marrow.org/)

From a personal perspective, one of my dear friends from high school was diagnosed with large cell B non-Hodgkin's lymphoma and needed to have a bone marrow transplant to put her cancer into remission. In her honor, I have dedicated this book to her.

I hope you enjoyed this story of hope and second chances. God always has a plan for us no matter how much we may try and fight it. While Elizabeth and Blake are fictitious, their fears, dreams and thoughts are something we can identify with. In our daily lives we are faced with many trials, but our faith helps us through those times because God is good.

I love to hear from my readers about how my books

have touched their lives. You can learn more about me and my books at www.kimwatters.com where you may also sign up for my periodic newsletter. Or you can write to me at Kim Watters, PO Box 4615, Cave Creek, AZ 85327.

Blessings,

Kim Watters

Questions for Discussion

1. From the beginning, Blake is uncertain about his ability to be a father because of his upbringing. Do you think he made the right choice in stepping forward right away to claim his daughter? What would you do if you were put in that same position?

2. Both Elizabeth and Blake are in professions that help other people. What do you do to help others?

3. Leukemia and all other types of cancers and illness are difficult to deal with. Why do you think God allows them to happen to His children?

4. Elizabeth believes she is following God's calling and doing His will on earth. What are some things you can do to serve God?

5. When Elizabeth has to share her daughter with Blake, what is her greatest fear? What is Blake's? How do they both deal with it? What is your greatest fear? How do you deal with it?

6. Blake turned away from God after the death of his mother when he was a child. Has there ever been a time in your life when you've questioned His plans for you? What did you do? How did you resolve your conflict?

7. Blake has a discussion with the pastor about God revealing himself to us. Can you name a time when God has revealed Himself to you or someone you know?

8. Blake has issues with how his father treated him in the past. How did it affect his life and his career choice? Have you ever had something happen to you in the past that affected choices you made? How did you handle it?

9. What is your favorite scene and why? What is your favorite character and why?

10. Elizabeth's faith helps her deal with her daughter's leukemia. Can you think of a time when you were down and God helped you through? How about how God works through your family and friends?

11. When Blake meets the pastor for the first time, he feels uncomfortable. Why? Have you ever been afraid or uncomfortable in a new situation? How did you handle it?

12. Read the quote from Isaiah at the beginning of the book. Can you think of a time in your life where this has applied to you? How did you handle it?

REQUEST YOUR FREE BOOKS!

2 FREE INSPIRATIONAL NOVELS
PLUS 2
FREE
MYSTERY GIFTS

Love Inspired

YES! Please send me 2 FREE Love Inspired® novels and my 2 FREE mystery gifts (gifts are worth about $10). After receiving them, if I don't wish to receive any more books, I can return the shipping statement marked "cancel." If I don't cancel, I will receive 6 brand-new novels every month and be billed just $4.49 per book in the U.S. or $4.99 per book in Canada. That's a saving of at least 22% off the cover price. It's quite a bargain! Shipping and handling is just 50¢ per book in the U.S. and 75¢ per book in Canada.* I understand that accepting the 2 free books and gifts places me under no obligation to buy anything. I can always return a shipment and cancel at any time. Even if I never buy another book, the two free books and gifts are mine to keep forever.

105/305 IDN FEGR

Name	(PLEASE PRINT)	
Address		Apt. #
City	State/Prov.	Zip/Postal Code

Signature (if under 18, a parent or guardian must sign)

Mail to the **Reader Service:**
IN U.S.A.: P.O. Box 1867, Buffalo, NY 14240-1867
IN CANADA: P.O. Box 609, Fort Erie, Ontario L2A 5X3

Not valid for current subscribers to Love Inspired books.

**Are you a subscriber to Love Inspired books
and want to receive the larger-print edition?
Call 1-800-873-8635 or visit www.ReaderService.com.**

* Terms and prices subject to change without notice. Prices do not include applicable taxes. Sales tax applicable in N.Y. Canadian residents will be charged applicable taxes. Offer not valid in Quebec. This offer is limited to one order per household. All orders subject to credit approval. Credit or debit balances in a customer's account(s) may be offset by any other outstanding balance owed by or to the customer. Please allow 4 to 6 weeks for delivery. Offer available while quantities last.

Your Privacy—The Reader Service is committed to protecting your privacy. Our Privacy Policy is available online at www.ReaderService.com or upon request from the Reader Service.

We make a portion of our mailing list available to reputable third parties that offer products we believe may interest you. If you prefer that we not exchange your name with third parties, or if you wish to clarify or modify your communication preferences, please visit us at www.ReaderService.com/consumerchoice or write to us at Reader Service Preference Service, P.O. Box 9062, Buffalo, NY 14269. Include your complete name and address.

LIREG11B

Love Inspired

TEXAS TWINS

Follow the adventures of two sets of twins who are torn apart by family secrets and learn to find their way home.

Her Surprise Sister by Marta Perry
July 2012

Mirror Image Bride by Barbara McMahon
August 2012

Carbon Copy Cowboy by Arlene James
September 2012

Look-Alike Lawman by Glynna Kaye
October 2012

The Soldier's Newfound Family
by Kathryn Springer
November 2012

Reunited for the Holidays
by Jillian Hart
December 2012

*Available wherever
books are sold.*

www.LoveInspiredBooks.com

LICONT0812

When a baby is left on the doorstep of an Amish house,
Sheriff Nick Bradley comes face-to-face with his past.

Read on for a preview of A HOME FOR HANNAH
by Patricia Davids.

The farmhouse door swung open before Sheriff Nick Bradley could knock. A woman with fiery auburn hair and green eyes stood glaring at him. "There has been a mistake. We don't need you here."

The shock of seeing Miriam Kauffman standing in front of him took him aback. He struggled to hide his surprise. It had been eight years since he'd laid eyes on her. A lifetime ago.

"Good morning to you, too, Miriam."

After all this time, she wasn't any better at hiding her opinion of him. She looked ready to spit nails. Proof that she hadn't forgiven him.

"Miriam, don't be rude," her mother chided. Miriam reluctantly stepped aside. He entered the house.

His cousin Amber sat at the table. "Hi, Nick. Thanks for coming. We do need your help."

Ada Kauffman sat across from her. The room was bathed in soft light from two kerosene lanterns hanging from hooks on the ceiling.

He glanced at the three women facing him. Ada Kauffman was Amish, from the top of her white prayer bonnet to the tips of her bare toes poking out from beneath her plain dress. Her daughter, Miriam, had never joined the church, choosing to leave before she was baptized. Her arms were crossed over her chest.

Amber served the Amish and non-Amish people of Hope Springs, Ohio, as a nurse midwife. Exactly what was she doing here?

He said, "Okay, I'm here. What's so sensitive that I had to come instead of sending one of my perfectly competent deputies?"

"This is why we called you." Amber gestured toward the basket. He took a step closer and saw a baby swaddled in the folds of a quilt.

"You called me here to see a new baby? Congratulations to whomever."

"Exactly," Miriam said.

He looked at her closely. "What am I missing?"

Amber said, "It's more about what we are missing."

"And that is?" he demanded.

Ada said, "A mother to go with this baby."

He shook his head. "You've lost me."

Miriam rolled her eyes. "I'm not surprised."

Her mother scowled at her, but said, "Someone left this baby on my porch."

*Will Nick and Miriam get past their differences
to help little Hannah?*

*Pick up A HOME FOR HANNAH by Patricia Davids,
available August 2012 from Love Inspired Books.*